CW00517713

FORCED TO KILL

EMMY ELLIS

CHAPTER ONE

Getting calls from the dead in the middle of the night wasn't Oliver Banks' idea of fun.

He stared down at the body resting in the mulch, the limbs at odd angles. Her blonde hair, splayed against a backdrop of soggy leaves, stood out starkly in the beam of his pencil-slim torch. Christ, what kind of people did this to another human being? Crazy bastards, that was who. Oliver had dealt with them before, had seen bodies like this too many times to count, and here he was again, lured out by the voices in his head and the unexplainable knowledge that someone had been murdered.

The woman, early thirties he reckoned, looked as though she'd been out walking. Mud-encrusted hiking boots, one tightly tied, the other undone, laces rigid, dried-out worm skins. Had the killer been interrupted in taking the boot off? And why the fuck would he have wanted to do that anyway?

Sometimes it was pointless questioning the idiosyncrasies of the warped. Sometimes they just did things. No reason. Just because.

He studied the woman's jeans. Mud splatters soiled the denim from the top of her boots to her thighs. Had she run through one of the many boggy areas in this godforsaken field? Had she tried to get away from the bastard who'd done this to her? Oliver hadn't been given any details other than the site and the fact that a dead body was there. He'd hauled his arse out of bed then dressed quickly, stuffing his hair under a beanie.

His battered trainers had sunk into the ground and would leave perfect imprints.

Fuck.

He shifted his gaze back to the woman, whose stomach was exposed, her black T-shirt bunched to just below her breasts. The perfect, taut skin showed the woman had taken care of herself, had maybe visited a gym regularly. What a damn waste

2

of a life. Her jacket, a black windbreaker, the fronts open, would have done nothing to keep off the winter chill. She had no hat or scarf, no gloves either, unless whoever had killed her had taken them away. Another oddity that wouldn't be a surprise. Killers took the strangest trophies.

There were no marks on her neck or face, no obvious signs of how she'd been killed. No bruising, no knife wounds, no blood. If it wasn't for her arms and legs clearly being broken, the woman might have appeared to have just fallen down and died.

He closed his eyes, aware morning would be here all too soon, that someone walking their dog might well discover the body. Or not. The recent rains had rendered this field a bit treacherous, and if she wasn't looked at soon by SOCO and another burst of rain lashed down, evidence would be washed away. Oliver had turned his ankle when traipsing over the ground, a hidden pothole that he'd called all the names under the sun. If anyone *chose* to walk here, they were mental.

"Were you mental walking here?" He directed his torch beam at the woman's face. "Or were you brought here?"

He swept an arc of light over the grass either side of the body. Yes, there they were in a patch of exposed mud, the footprints of the victim and also someone else, who had a larger size, undoubtedly those of a man. And it was always a man, wasn't it? At least it had been in Oliver's experience. The grass was trampled so much in places it had been

3

ripped up. The footprints, prominent in a muddy swathe, were dotted about, but a mass of them, like two people had stood together and tussled.

"So you put up a fight." Oliver hunkered down and studied the woman's nails. Pristine, acrylic, long. "But it seems you didn't get to scratch him. That's a bit of a shit, isn't it?"

Female laughter echoed inside his head, delicate and sweet. At last, she'd made contact again. He'd been waiting for it, had thought the victim would never break through a second time, but there she was, giggling.

"What kept you?" Oliver asked, saddened that once again he'd be speaking to someone he'd never get to meet in life. Someone who'd never use her body to help express herself. Someone who'd been snuffed out because another human being had decided on it. "Fucking arsehole."

The giggle came again, then a sigh. Then a sob.
Shit.

"You can see yourself here?"

Oliver sensed her spirit had just caught up with the recent events. She'd realised she was dead, left in a field for someone to find or for a wild animal to feast on. Or to rot, never to be seen again, unless you counted bones. Not something anyone envisaged for themselves at the best of times, but there it was, a bold, vile fact of life. Sometimes people got offed and didn't get a decent burial.

"Sorry if you heard my thoughts there. I need to work on my empathy skills. Work on keeping you out when I'm thinking shit like that." Oliver switched off his torch, suddenly unable to look at the body now her spirit was with him. It wasn't just a body anymore but a person, one who was in his mind and would hopefully help him track the killer. "Listen, you can either stay here or find somewhere else to be, but if you reach out, I'll be listening. If you want me to help, I can. It's just that..." He glanced at the horizon, obscured by a line of gnarly, leafless trees. "I have to call this in so the coppers can get you out of this place. Your body, I mean. You? You're free to go wherever you want."

Oliver slid his torch in his jeans back pocket. Fuck, what he'd give to be normal, to have his mind to himself.

He'd burn his trainers, buy a new pair. As usual. He hated wearing them after he'd been to a scene.

This malarky was getting expensive.

He walked across the grass towards his car parked on a verge beside the trees that lined the edge of the field. He'd ring DI Langham, speak with him, then go home, get rid of his shoes, shower, catch a bit more sleep. Or maybe, if he was lucky, the dead woman would contact him and they could get to the real work of finding the wanker who'd done this.

In his car, he gunned the engine then switched the heat on, letting the vehicle idle along with his thoughts. Daylight might be on the cusp of arriving in a few hours, but shit, he had to take a moment to compartmentalise what he'd seen, file away the insignificant and concentrate on the important.

The woman had struggled, so she'd known she was in trouble. Did she know her killer? He hadn't thought to *fully* check the area, to see if there were two tracks side by side in the grass leading up to the final resting place or whether there was just one. Was she followed or with someone? Had she willingly gone with this bloke or been forced?

"This is where you come in, love," he muttered, cocking his head, waiting for a response. Nothing. "All right, so you don't want to talk."

Oliver shielded his thoughts. The woman didn't need to know he was pissed off at his lack of attention to detail, that he'd failed her already with his incompetence. He'd been doing this long enough to know the drill by now. Scope the area and find out as much as he could without disturbing the body. Get clues, anything to help him find the sick shit. Still, she'd made contact again, that was the main thing, and he'd have to be content with that.

He glanced at the rearview mirror and frowned. Was that another vehicle behind? Turning in his seat, he stared out of the back window. It was hard to tell whether it was a car or just a dark mound, a part of the verge. He hadn't taken any notice when he'd arrived, hadn't bloody concentrated. What was up with him?

A light flickered, right about where a windscreen would be, and Oliver's stomach muscles bunched. Was that an interior light going on, then off? Had someone struck a match or lighter? He waited, breath held, for the light to appear again. His car engine hummed—he wanted to get the fuck home. If someone was out there, he didn't fancy meeting with them.

A shiver went down his back, and the hairs on his neck stood on end.

He gritted his teeth and pulled out his phone. Seemed he did this too often lately. The calls from the dead were becoming more frequent, and as soon as one case was solved and closed, another came along. He dialled a number he knew by heart and waited for the pick-up.

"DI Langham."

"Um, it's me."

A sigh, then, "All right. What have you got?"

"Dead body."

"Now there's a surprise. Where?"

"The field on the Keach Road turnoff. Female. About thirty."

"Right." Another sigh. "Wait for me there."

"I can't."

"Why the fuck not?" Langham getting testy wasn't a good thing.

"Because there's a car parked a few metres behind me."

"Jesus fucking Christ, Oliver. Would you *stop* visiting the bloody sites? Just ring me when you get the information."

"I can't help it. I have to visit. It's how I connect. How I get the information that helps *you* break the case and makes *you* look like a sodding hero."

"Fuck you."

"So, are you coming out here or what?"

"I'd like to say 'or what' but—"

"Do I wait here or go home?"

"Wait. See if the car moves."

"And if it does? You want me to follow it?"

"Fuck, no. Just take the number plate."

"Right."

"I'm just getting in my car."

Oliver looked in the rearview again. The light flickered once more, and headlights burst into life. His guts twisted.

"Um…"

"What?"

"The car's ready to go."

"Shit. I'm ten minutes away. Get the plate."

"What if it goes the other way?"

The car nosed onto the road.

Bollocks. "Um, it's heading towards me."

"Good, sit tight."

"No. I mean, it's heading *towards* me. *For* me."

"Then get out of there!"

Oliver wedged the phone between his shoulder and ear and eased onto the rain-slicked road, headlamps on low beam, rapiers of light cutting into the darkness. A quick glance in the mirror told him the car was gaining on him at speed. He accelerated, hoping to make it to the farmhouse standing in the distance. It had lights on, creamy squares of hominess that called to Oliver, had him wanting a normal life with a family who gave a shit whether he lived and breathed. His? They'd cast him out the minute he'd hit eighteen, telling him never to bring his weird arse back because he wasn't right in the head. Yeah, well, they ought to try living like he had for as far back as he could remember. Having dead people in his bloody head, asking for help, taking him places he'd never thought he'd go. Seeing things he'd never thought he'd see. Having mad people follow him in their cars in the middle of the pissing night.

He pushed his foot down on the accelerator.

"Give me an update," Langham said.

"Whoever it is...let's just say they know I've seen them. They're right up my arse. I'm driving west. Farmhouse ahead. The road bends, leads to—"

"Crooks Lane. Yeah, I know where you are. I've just turned onto Keach," Langham said. "Couple of minutes away. Road's long. Uniforms will be here in a bit, but not in time to deal with this fucker. What's going on?"

Oliver eyed the mirror. "The car's *right* up my jacksy."

"Uncomfortable."

"Very fucking funny."

"The farmhouse?"

"Still too far away."

A smack to the back of Oliver's car had him shunting forward. "Shit! *Shit!*"

"What? What's happening?"

"He's dinged my bumper."

"Well, drive faster!"

Oliver shook his head and pelted down the road, creating space between his car and the other. Adrenaline flowed faster, and he coached himself calmer, only to have his nerves jangle as the car pulled across and sped up, riding alongside him.

"He's next to me, Langham."

"Yeah, I'm a good way back but I see your taillights."

Oliver glanced sideways. The driver stared at him.

"Um, Langham?"

"Yep?"

"You know I said *he'd* dinged my bumper?"

"Yeah…"

"Make that a she."

"What?"

"Yeah. Some bird. Black hair."

The other car suddenly slewed towards Oliver's, the side of it crashing into his. He tightened his grip on the steering wheel and focused on the road ahead, driving faster in an attempt to get away.

"Shit," Langham said.

A siren split the air, and a blue strobe illuminated the interior of Oliver's car. He looked at the mad driver, the woman's face clearer now. Her hands clearer—great big hands that had no business being on a female. After checking the road ahead, Oliver stared back at the car.

"It's a mask," Oliver said. "The driver's wearing a mask and wig."

"Yeah, and that driver's going to be moving pretty fast away from me any…second…now."

The driver didn't. The car bashed into Oliver's again, an almighty whack that jolted him across the road and onto the verge. The uneven ground beneath his tyres made for a bumpy ride, and he struggled to control his vehicle. Panic threatened to overtake, and he fought to remain alert, on target.

"Oliver, watch yourself."

"I'm trying!"

"There's a tree ahead. Move over. Now!"

"Can't you see the other car's stopping me?"

The tree loomed up ahead, and Oliver yanked the wheel, hoping to make it past the wide trunk in time. He did, but his front tyre clipped an exposed root, and his car overturned, rattling his teeth and bones. His head smacked the side window, dislodging his phone. The car kept on rolling, and Langham's voice, tinny and distant, came out of his mobile, wherever the fuck it had fallen.

"Follow her," Oliver shouted. "Or him. Don't worry about me. Just go."

His car came to a lurching stop. Upside down. He hung, hands still on the wheel, heart beating like a bitch with a score to settle. And shit, he had a score to settle now. Not only did he have a killer to catch, but someone who had also tried to kill him—*and* pissed him off into the bargain.

When his car had spun, one of his fingers had broken.

And *that* was enough to have him seeing red.

CHAPTER TWO

No one broke his finger and got away with it. Oliver grimaced. Not only had it broken, but the nail had been ripped off way below the level of acceptability. Fuck, did his fingertip hurt. His temple throbbed. Hitting it on a window would do that. He'd bet he had a lump the size of an egg beside his eye.

Assessing his situation, he glanced around and sniffed. It didn't smell like any petrol had leaked, but he wasn't hanging around long enough to find out. But he was hanging, held in place by his seat belt. He unclipped it, bracing for another bang to the head as he dropped to the ceiling. Annoyed, he reached for the door and fumbled with the lock, expecting fate to play games with him and trap him inside. Thankfully, the door opened, just not enough for him to climb out. He was slim, but a size below small he was not.

With anger and frustration simmering, he clambered across the passenger seat and opened that door. It swung wide with a groan from the hinges, then a pair of legs appeared. He tensed until he spotted familiar brown loafers.

"I told you to follow the driver." Oliver craned his neck to get a look at the DI.

Langham stared down at him, a tousle-headed blond with a face that showed no signs he'd been woken out of a deep sleep. Bastard. He did frown, though, which was something.

"The uniforms are on it. Do you want some help getting out, or will my offer end with bullshit from your foul mouth?"

Oliver almost laughed. Almost. Langham knew him too well. "I'll try and get out myself, and if I can't, *then* you can help me."

"Stubborn twat."

Oliver scrabbled out on hands and knees, the grass cold and wet, soaking through his jeans. He stood and brushed himself off, ignoring the lightheadedness and the throb of his finger, his head. "So other coppers are covering that arsehole."

"Yeah." Langham scrubbed his chin, the rasp of his stubble loud despite Oliver's car engine still growling. "I got the number plate. Good job I did, seeing as *you* didn't."

Oliver widened his eyes. "You had better be joking."

"Yeah, I'm joking. Lighten up. Anyone would think you'd just had a car accident."

Oliver walked away, leaving *him* to switch off the engine. *Let him blow himself up.* Langham riled Oliver as often as he could, and most times he could handle it, gave as good as Langham gave him, but now? Here? No, this wasn't fucking funny. He'd find the person who'd made him break a finger if it bloody killed him.

"And maybe it will," he muttered and, looking over his shoulder, he called, "And get my phone, will you?"

He climbed up the embankment, finding himself at the side of the road where he'd veered off course. He'd been so close to the farmhouse. Lifting his hand, he touched his temple, careful in his exploration. The last thing he needed was pain. He didn't bear it well. It felt as though he had a simple contusion, one that would shrink within a couple of days.

His engine died, then Langham came up behind him. He took his elbow and turned Oliver to face him. His frown was back. Good.

14

"This is why I ask you not to visit sites." Langham stared. "It's too dangerous."

"Yeah, well, we've been through this before. I can't not come. You don't understand."

"I do, but you got hurt this time, and I warned you something like this would happen."

"Yep, but it's done now. No point going on about it." He smiled to ease the acid in his tone. "So, what next?"

"I do what I do, you do what you do. Follow the pattern. It's never failed in the past."

"Right. Could I get a lift home?" Oliver turned away to walk towards Langham's car. "It's a long way, and I'm fucked if I have the energy to make it."

"You need a doctor first." Langham placed Oliver's phone in his hand.

"No thanks. And cheers for getting my phone." He climbed inside and settled in the passenger seat, staring down the embankment at his trusty little Fiat that wasn't so trusty anymore. Christ knew how much it would cost to get it fixed.

Langham joined him, starting the engine. "I can't take you back just yet, though."

"Oh. Yeah."

"I need to get to the murder site, maybe get another officer to take you home when they arrive. You'll have questions to answer before that, though."

"Yeah. Good job they know I'm a whacko who can be trusted. Otherwise... Shit, I'm not even going there."

15

"Best you don't."

Langham drove down the road in silence, leaving Oliver to work out exactly what he was going to say in his statement. The police knew what he did, what he was, and at first had suspected *him* of killing people. He could see how they'd arrived at that conclusion, him always knowing where the bodies were, but when he'd given them information the victims had told him, leading them to the killers, and had proven alibis for himself, he'd been let off the hook. Now they approached *him* for help, but it didn't work like that. He couldn't just summon the dead and bombard them with questions. He had to be contacted by them, and sometimes the dead just didn't want to speak.

Once, he'd been taken down into the morgue to try to get information from an old duffer who'd been found stabbed to death in his home. The grey-haired fella hadn't been in the mood for chatting, had told Oliver to fuck off and mind his own business, and he had. Gladly. He never had been good with the elderly.

Langham pulled over, parking close to where Oliver had earlier. Another shiver abseiled down his spine, and he took a moment to wonder whether it was the return to the scene that spooked him or whether the victim teetered on contacting him. He concentrated, sensing nothing but his own thoughts inside his mind. The woman would speak when she felt like it and not before.

Langham cut the engine. "You ready to show me where she is?"

"Yeah."

With protective booties on, they strode across the field, Oliver watching out for potholes. He contemplated telling Langham to do the same, but seeing him fall arse over tit was an amusing concept. Oliver led the way, the shape of the body clearer now the sky had lightened a little. Not much, but enough to show her whereabouts. He stopped in the same place as before and stared at her.

Something was different.

He narrowed his eyes and reached into his back pocket, relieved his torch was still there. Switching it on, he aimed the beam at the woman's T-shirt. It had been clean before, just a black top. Now, what appeared to be sugar strands peppered the fabric, the kind that were sprinkled on iced doughnuts. What the fuck?

"Um, they weren't here before." He nodded at the multicoloured specks.

"What weren't?"

"The sugar strands. On her T-shirt. Fuck." It dawned on him that someone had been here as he'd walked across the field to his car. It had to have been the person in that other vehicle. Had it been parked there when he'd arrived and he just hadn't seen it? "I'd swear that car wasn't there when I got here, but now I'm not so sure."

"It might not have been."

Oliver turned to face Langham. "What, it might have come along after?"

"Yep. How long were you here?"

"A while. Half an hour?"

"Right. Maybe the killer forgot to put those strands on her and came back. No maybe about it—it's obvious that's what happened. What did you do when you got in your car?"

"I switched on the engine and had a little think."

"A little think. Okay... How long for?"

Oliver tried to estimate the time. "I don't know. Five minutes?"

"And you noticed the car when?"

"I turned on the engine, glanced in the mirror."

"Okay. Then what?"

"I saw a light."

"Which could have been...?"

"The driver getting back in the car. Shit."

"Yes, shit. You were lucky he didn't bloody come for you. So, in future, will you at least ring me and let me know you're going to a site, and wait for me to go with you?"

Oliver nodded. Langham was right. He shouldn't be doing this crap alone.

"Good," Langham said. "Now then, do you notice anything else different about her?"

Oliver flashed his beam over the woman once more. It pissed him off that he didn't know her name yet, but that would come in time—*if* she decided to tell him.

Oh God. Her boots had been removed.

"Shit. When I was last here, she had boots on. Hiking boots. One was tied tight, the other untied." Dread pooled in his stomach. "I interrupted the killer, didn't I, by turning up?" He glanced at Langham.

He nodded. "Seems that way. And that's something that hasn't happened before. Have you felt different lately? Like your ability is evolving?"

Oliver shook his head. "No, I feel the same. She called me like the others did. Woke me, said... Oh Jesus."

"What?"

"She said she was *being* killed, not that she was dead. I didn't... I just didn't think anything of it. I got up as usual and came out here after she told me where to go. Then nothing." He swallowed. "So I got here and waited for her to speak to me, and she did. Well, she never said anything, just laughed at something I said or thought, can't remember now, and then... Then she realised she was dead and hasn't spoken since."

Langham lifted a hand and rested it on Oliver's shoulder. "How long did it take you to get here?"

"I don't know. Ten minutes? Maybe twenty? Shitty traffic diversions." And all that time, while Oliver had travelled without any rush, this woman had been fighting for her life. "Fuck it!"

"You weren't to know. This is a first for you." Langham dropped his hand to his side.

Oliver eyed the corpse. "So I disturbed the killer, and what? He ran off? Waited in the fucking bushes while I stood here? Went off and got his

19

bloody car to waste some time until I'd finished? He took a risk, didn't he? I could have called you right away." He slapped an open palm to his thigh and turned away, looking out onto the road. "Your buddies are here."

"Ignore them. Is there anything else different?"

Reluctantly, Oliver slowly spun around. "Yes. Her legs are straight. They were at odd angles before. Her arms, too." He studied her some more. "And fuck me, but her stomach wasn't anything like that."

"Like what?"

"Split open and bleeding. It was normal. I remember thinking she must have liked the gym because it was so toned."

"And that's all?"

Oliver panned the torch beam farther up. *Oh Jesus Christ...* "No, that's *not* all. Last time she had a face."

What the hell had he stumbled on this time? It had been bad enough seeing the woman as she had been, let alone how she was now.

He faced the road again. Several officers navigated their way across the grass. One, DS Shields, in his usual impeccable suit, bugged the shit out of him, and he closed his eyes momentarily to quell the irritation. He was an arrogant twat who tolerated Oliver, was one of the many who'd scoffed at his ability in the beginning. The one who was still a thorn in his side and made no bones about the fact that he thought Oliver had been involved in all the murders so far. Just that he couldn't prove it.

What an arsehole.

He stopped in front of Oliver, eyes narrowed, the look on his face telling him he suspected him yet again. "Ah, so it's one of *yours*, is it?" he said, lacing his hands in front of him and rocking on the balls of his feet. "Might have known when Langham called it in."

"Whatever. You think what you like. This has nothing to do with me." Oliver presented his back to him; it would piss the bastard off.

"So…" Shields moved to stand between Oliver and Langham. "What do we have here?"

Langham cleared his throat. "Oliver was called out and—"

Shields chuckled. "Called out. I just love the way you use that term."

"Oliver was called out, and it seems he disturbed the killer this time."

"Is that right?" Shields jabbed Oliver in the ribs.

"Yes."

"So it isn't that someone disturbed *you?*" Shields tilted his head and stared at Oliver, a little too hard for his liking.

"No, I wasn't disturbed. I came out, as usual, saw her here, and went back to my car to ring Langham."

He related what had followed, ignoring Shields' look of disbelief and the sneer on his fleshy lips. His dark, slicked-back hair was rigid, like he'd doused it with a can of hairspray prior to coming

out, and he stank of freshly applied aftershave—
the cheap kind that cost a couple of quid on the
market.

Oliver held back a snort. "And then we came
back and found her like this."

"I see." Shields squatted, hands draped between
his open knees. "So, let's go with what you've said.
Let's say you're telling the truth. Now ask this poor
bitch who did it and save us a lot of hassle."

Oliver sighed and flared his nostrils. "You know
it doesn't work like that."

"Convenient," Shields said. "Gives your
accomplices time to get away. I mean, think about
it." He rose and towered above him. "These dead
people never seem to speak to you again until a
couple of days after they've been killed. Now why
is that?"

"Maybe they need time to adjust. Maybe they
have to pass over to wherever the fuck they go to
when they die. I don't know. And I don't
appreciate your tone."

"I don't care what you appreciate, Mr Banks. I
don't care about anything but arresting you."

"That's enough!" Langham stepped between
them. "You know damn well Oliver isn't involved
in this shit, and it isn't something you should be
discussing out here anyway. We have work to do, a
scene to secure, evidence to find before it pisses
down. Arguing halts the process. Let Oliver do his
thing and you do yours."

"Testy," Shields said, crouching at the victim's feet again. "So what did she look like before she had her face sliced off?"

"Pretty. Like a doll." Oliver said.

"You can give a description?" Shields rounded his shoulders.

"Of course I can."

"Christ, you're testy, too. What's up with the pair of you?"

"You," Oliver snapped, stalking away so he could be alone. At the road, he leant against Langham's car. God, if he killed anyone, it would be Shields.

A giggle echoed inside his head.

Thank fuck!

"Hey, you," Oliver said. "How're you doing?"

No response.

"Can I at least have a name? Yours? His?"

"I don't know him."

"Oh, right. Any clue as to why he chose you?"

"Something to do with work."

"Which is?"

"PrivoLabs."

"Ah. Are you a scientist?"

"No. A secretary."

"And he works there?"

"No."

"But he knows someone who does?"

"Maybe."

Oliver rolled his eyes. "Love, you need to be a bit more specific."

"Yes, he must do. I... I knew something."

"And…?"

"He shut me up."

"What did you know?"

"I can't tell you. He said if I told you—"

"I don't want to rub it in here, but you're dead. He can't hurt you anymore, so if you tell me—"

"No, he knows about you. He said he'd looked you up in his car. Your number plate, on his laptop. If I tell you anything, he'll hurt my son."

"He knows about me?"

"Yes, he said if I thought about telling the psychic after I'm gone, he'd know. I can't… I made you find me, that was enough. And he knows. He came back after you went to your car."

"I noticed."

"He said then that if I told you anything else…"

"I see."

"I have to go."

"No, wait! What's with the sugar strands?"

"I can't tell you. I'm sorry, but I just can't. My son…"

"Shit!" Oliver made his way back to the scene. Once there, he caught Langham's attention and repeated the latest news.

"So we have something, at least." Langham pinched his chin between finger and thumb. "PrivoLabs. You fancy coming along with me?"

"Yeah. After I've showered and got rid of these trainers."

"Ah, yes, the shoe thing. Okay. Let's go."

CHAPTER THREE

The sun had brightened the sky and chased away the darkness of the last few hours, but it hadn't erased the visuals from Oliver's mind. No, they'd remain there until this case was over, until he could file them in a box labelled FORGET, although that never really worked. Still, he tried to put solved cases to the back of his mind, told himself the dead were at peace once he'd helped them, and that was all he could do. A person could only do so much. He couldn't force them to move on, could only block them out to make way for new ones. And shit, he wished there were never any new ones. Wished no one had to die the way they did.

In clean clothing and freshly showered, he stared up at the PrivoLabs building, Langham beside him. Sunlight bounced off the too-many-to-count, blue-tinted windows. The structure stretched into the air, an accusing finger, the roof obscured by puffy clouds that spoke of snow on the way. Fucking brilliant. With no car, he'd be forced to walk everywhere, and he didn't own a pair of boots suitable for that sort of weather. He'd have to buy some when he went to shop for some new trainers.

"You ready?" Langham asked, walking up the grey marble steps to the double-wide glass front doors.

"As I'll ever be."

Langham pushed one door open and held it so Oliver could step inside. Allowing it to close behind them, he muttered, "As usual, keep your mouth shut, your eyes open, and your mind tuned for the victim to contact you."

"Her name is Louise, not 'the victim'."

Shields had secured an ID, informing them of her identity as they'd driven through the city towards PrivoLabs. He'd also made sure Louise's son was in a secure place under protection, with Louise's mother.

They approached the reception desk, and Langham gently cleared his throat. He leant on the polished wood and asked to see the manager, flashing his ID to a startled receptionist, who nodded and lifted the phone handset to her ear. Oliver left him to it, idly glancing around to get a feel for the place. The glass walls appeared clear, nothing like the blue they were outside. Leather sofas dotted the area, black and plush, and if he wasn't here for any reason but to crash out, he'd climb on one of them and sleep the sleep of the dead. He mentally cursed himself for his turn of phrase and eyed the many potted plants, tall ferns, and coconut palms, the leaves thick enough to hide a person. This outfit must rake in the money.

"Oliver?"

He turned at the sound of Langham's voice and walked towards him. "Are we off to do some questioning then?"

"Um, we would be if Louise had worked here and we had any tangible evidence something was amiss."

"What?"

"She never worked here, Oliver."

"But she said—"

"I know what she said, but there isn't any record of her ever being here. Are you sure she said she actually worked *here?*"

Oliver thought back. "Well, no. She said she was killed because of something to do with work, then mentioned PrivoLabs. Shit. Sorry." Something had been way off ever since Louise had woken him with the first call. His lack of concentration. Missing crucial information, like whether cars were parked on the side of the damn road. And now there was another misdemeanour to add to his growing list. He'd misinterpreted what Louise had said, bringing them out on a trip they needn't have made.

"Can't we question the manager anyway? Didn't you check my information first? Didn't Shields confirm where she worked when he looked her up?"

"No. Your information is usually correct, so we didn't—"

"Ah. Right. My fault. My fuck-up is going to go down *so* well with Shields. He'll gloat like the bastard he is."

"Fuck Shields."

Oliver stormed out of the building, angry. Was he losing his touch? It wouldn't be so bad if he didn't have to deal with this kind of thing—the voices, the messages. Maybe he just needed sleep, a solid few hours where he wasn't interrupted.

Langham came up behind him. "Listen, don't beat yourself up. Shit happens."

"Yeah, it usually does to me, but not like this."

"Anything on your mind?" He steered Oliver towards his car and opened the passenger door, ushering him inside.

Oliver stared up at him from the seat. "That's a stupid question. One of the worst you've come out with. There's *always* something on my mind."

He smiled. "Not like that. Not the voices. I mean worries. Stuff you need to talk about."

"What, like me messing up? No, I don't want to talk about that." He stared out of the windscreen, jaw rigid, hands bunched into fists in his lap. "Are you going to stand there staring at me for much longer? I mean, it's cold out, and the door being open..."

Langham climbed in then peeled away from the kerb.

"So, what next?" Oliver asked.

"We go back to the station and find out where the victim—"

"Louise."

"The *victim* worked. Then we go from there."

"Why don't you ever call them by their names?" Oliver looked across at him.

"Because then it becomes personal. I don't do personal."

They spent the remainder of the journey in silence. As soon as the car drew to a stop, Oliver hauled arse, striding towards the station with purpose. He shoved the door open then made his way towards Langham's office. There, he slumped into the chair and plonked his feet on the desk, crossing his legs at the ankles. His head itched, and he snatched off his beanie, tossing it across the room.

Langham walked in and eyed him from the doorway. "Why do you always insist on doing that?"

"Doing what?" he asked, picking at a hangnail.

"Sitting in my chair with your feet on my desk. Look, you're scrunching my papers."

Oliver planted his feet on the floor and scooted the chair across the room, picking up his hat so he had something to occupy his hands.

"You two make a good team."

Oliver sat upright, startled that Louise had decided to contact him now. "Hey, Louise. You all right?"

Langham raised his eyebrows, and Oliver put a finger to his lips so he'd remain quiet.

"I'm okay."

"So, we went to PrivoLabs and found out you didn't work there. Do you want to tell me where you did work?" Oliver closed his eyes, bouncing his heels and hoping for a positive answer.

"He said—"

"I know, love, but it doesn't matter what you tell me now. Your son is safe."

"He is?"

"Yes. He's living with your mother."

"My mother? Oh no...not her..."

"What's up with that? You two not get along? She's all your son has now, he has nowhere else to go. We've moved them both to a secure location. He won't find them."

"Oh God. He'll know she has him."

30

"It's okay. Don't worry about that. He won't find them. Can you tell me what you know?"

"I'd been filing, and a piece of paper fell out. I shouldn't have looked, should have just put it back inside the folder, but I held about three and wasn't sure which one it came from. So I read it and saw..."

Oliver waited a few beats. Louise didn't continue, so he prompted, "Saw...?"

"They're doing experiments."

"Who are?"

"PrivoLabs."

"Yep, that's what they do."

"Yes, but these ones... What I read were notes. They probably weren't even meant to be in the file. Handwritten."

"So what are they doing? What tests are they?"

"They're drugging children."

Oliver jumped up from the chair and paced. Langham grabbed a notebook and pen from his desk and held them out to him, but Oliver waved them away.

"With what?" His heart pattered fast, and he felt sick to his stomach.

"With this stuff. Like... God, you're not going to believe me. She didn't..."

"Try me."

"With this stuff to make them do things."

"Do things?"

"Yes. Bad things. They want to see whether the drugs make the children kill. I never thought... I never suspected..."

31

"What?" Oliver stilled, bile in his throat and a sour feeling in his gut. This kind of shit didn't happen, did it?

"He's taken the drugs, too. The man who..."

"Have you got a name?"

"I don't know it."

"What about the name of the person who wrote the notes."

"No."

"So how did anyone find out what you knew?"

"I gave the note to my boss."

"And what happened then?"

"He started an investigation. Got PrivoLabs' attention with it. He got sacked."

"What's his name?"

"Mr Reynolds. Mark Reynolds."

"Right, thank you. Anything else you can remember?"

"He...ah, he came to my house."

"Who, Reynolds?"

"No, the man. The man who killed me."

"Right." Confused as fuck was the order of the moment.

"He told me I had to go with him, leave my son asleep. And he said if I didn't, he'd give my lad that stuff. The sugar strands."

"Okay. Do you want to talk about what he did to you?"

"Not really."

"But can you at least tell me something about him so we can catch him?"

"He was tall. Very tall. Big hands. He had a smell..."

"What of?"

"Musty clothing. Like he lived in a dirty place."

"What did he look like?"

"I don't know. He wore a mask and a wig."

So it *was* that fucker who'd tried to run Oliver off the road. If he'd been given shit to make him kill, it explained why he'd been intent on crashing into Oliver's car. Why he'd killed Louise...although he'd clearly had another reason for getting rid of her. Louise had been in the wrong place at the wrong time, discovering something she shouldn't have—and look where it had got her. Oliver wondered about the virtues of being honest and doing the right thing. Sometimes it was best to just keep your mouth shut.

"I wish I had."

"Sorry, Louise. I didn't mean for you to hear that."

"It's okay."

"No, it's not."

"I'm tired. This is hard work."

"I know. Can you try for one last bit of information for me? Something about him that stands out? Louise? Louise, are you there?" Oliver strained for a response, a whisper, anything.

Silence.

"Fuck it!"

"Has she gone?" Langham asked.

"Yes." Oliver flopped back into the chair, rage bubbling inside him over thoughts of the hateful

33

things people did to others. Killing. Hurting. What the hell was *wrong* with them? Why did they feel the need to *do* shit like that?

"So, when you're ready..." Langham took a folding chair from against the wall and set it up behind his desk. He rested his elbows on his blotter, steepled his long fingers, and propped his chin on the tips.

"Give me a second." Oliver jammed his fingers in his hair. "I need to remember everything she said. I don't need another fuck-up on my résumé."

Langham failed at stifling a sigh.

"Have you got a problem with that?" Oliver snapped.

"No, but it seems you do."

"I don't *do* wrong, okay? I don't *do* fucking up."

"I know, and you don't usually, so cut yourself some slack, will you? Concentrate on what she told you, tell me, and then we can get the ball rolling."

CHAPTER FOUR

Langham stared at Oliver, one eyebrow raised, and took his elbows off the desk. "So, we're talking some strange shit here. If the victim's meant to be believed, this bloke took something that *made* him kill?" He sighed then stood, gazing at some spot or other on the carpet, pinching his chin.

"Is there something more interesting than this case in the carpet pile?" Oliver asked, frustrated and angrier than he'd been in a long while.

Louise had given just enough information to make him want to catch this fucker quickly, catch the people doing those experiments. Using sugar strands was ingenious, lacing food with them, food kids liked to eat. Where were they distributing these doughnuts or whatever the fuck they put the strands on? A shop? Free on some stall? In PrivoLabs itself?

Langham's apparent lack of concern, his almost languid perusal of worn-down carpet fibres, pissed Oliver right off.

"I mean," Oliver said, "there's only Louise to consider here. Only a dead woman who died because she knew something she shouldn't. Only a kid left without a mother—a kid currently in hiding with his gran, who has to put aside her grieving to make sure she does everything right for the lad. Only a load of other kids and their parents suffering at the hands of some mental bastards." He stood abruptly and paced again. "You're getting on my fucking nerves staring at the floor like that."

Langham gave Oliver a dark look—one of the darkest he'd ever been given. "I'll ignore that outburst. Put it down to you being tired and overprotective of the victim. Distraught over the kids being plied with drugs. Staring into space helps me—"

"Overprotective? Over-fucking-protective? Are you deliberately trying to rile me?" Oliver moved to the door and curled his hand around the knob, his intent to storm out. Langham wouldn't solve this case as fast without him, and Oliver had a mind to follow the leads himself. Anything to get something done *now*.

Langham sighed. "Listen, you're flying high on adrenaline, with the need to get to the bottom of this, but you know it doesn't work like that. You get like this every time, and every time I tell you the same thing. Slow down. Think things through. And we'll get there. We always do."

"You're right," Oliver said. "As usual."

"So, someone's feeding people drugs that make them kill, someone who wears a wig and mask. So what now?"

"How do I fucking know? I need Louise to come back, tell me more."

"And that might be in the next few minutes, an hour, three days, or not at all. We can't rely on her. Got to do something ourselves."

"I know that. We've got other information to go on. PrivoLabs doing experiments on kids. They're somehow getting children to eat food with sugar strands on them. Where are the drugs being kept?"

"That's a bit delicate, going to Privo," Langham said. "We can't just storm in there and demand they show us their experiment records."

"Why not?"

"We don't have proof they're doing anything, so we can't get a warrant. Use your head. All we have is some dead woman's word."

Langham had a point, but Oliver believed Louise, knew she was telling the truth.

"We do have proof. That bloke left those strands on Louise's body."

Langham snatched up the phone and barked orders to some unfortunate on the other end. He slammed the receiver down. "Forensics will be on it...when they're on it. No sense of bloody haste, that lot."

"So, while we wait, we interview Mark Reynolds. Who's the fucking detective here, me or you?"

"Sod off. Come on, we have someone to ask a shitload of questions."

CHAPTER FIVE

Out of the office and in Langham's car, Oliver was more focused. Unease at interviewing a bloke who might not want to answer their questions had him shifting in his seat. What if Reynolds had been threatened to keep quiet? What if Langham had to haul his arse into the police station in order to get some answers? Even then the man might not play ball. Fright would keep his mouth shut.

Langham drove out of the city, their journey taking them to some out-of-the-way place called Lower Repton Oliver had only heard of but not visited. A tiny hamlet wasn't his ideal destination, but he was pleasantly surprised by the quaintness of the area. Cottages flanked the roadside, and a small, Cotswold stone pub, Pickett's Inn, sat hunched on the bend in the road, a decrepit old man, its roof bowed, walls bulging outwards.

Oliver shuddered. The place might be quaint, but something was off here. He sensed many spirits lurking nearby and imagined there *would* be a fair few, what with the hamlet being so old. People would have lived here all their lives, dying in their beds.

"Um, which cottage is his?" he asked, anxious to get this interview over and done with. "I don't like it here."

"Me neither. Maybe it's the remoteness, but I wouldn't live here if you paid me." Langham leant forward over the steering wheel and peered at the cottages. "None of them are numbered, just named. Reynolds' records said he lives at number two, but it's anyone's guess which end of the road that is."

"You could get out and ask." Oliver nodded at an elderly woman in her front garden, nosing at what they were doing, no doubt. She held a watering can, which she'd tipped as though she'd really come out to wet the plants—*at this time of year?*—except no water drizzled from the spout. "Bet she'll know which one we're after."

Langham drew up to the roadside outside the woman's aged, wooden fence and wound down his window. "Excuse me, which house is number two?"

She squinted and ground her unquestionably false teeth, wispy strands of white hair escaping her bun. Her lips looked elasticated, undulating like that. "What you want to know for? Who are you?"

"I'm DI Langham," he said, whipping out his ID and showing her. "And I need to speak to the resident. Mark Reynolds?"

"Ain't seen him. Not since the last copper came along to speak to him, and *he* was familiar. Like I'd seen him before somewhere."

Oliver's stomach clenched. "Something's off. I feel it."

"You and me both," Langham said, then to the woman, "Another policeman was here?"

"Yes, I just said so, didn't I?" She *tsked* and rolled her eyes. "No idea how you people solve crimes if you can't even process a simple sentence. Yes, another policeman. ID just like yours. And Mark lives back there. Second one in on the other side of the road." She marched down her path towards her cottage, turning to stare at them when she reached her front door.

"Thank the Lord for nosy old bitches, but fuck me," Langham muttered.

"Let's interview this bloke and get out of here. This place... There are too many ghosts here. They're all trying to speak to me."

41

Langham made a U-turn in the deserted road. "So let them in. Maybe we'll learn something."

Oliver widened his eyes. "Are you serious? You try having a few of them gossiping in your head all at once."

Langham parked outside number two, the wooden plaque beside the front door announcing the cottage as Reynolds' Gaff.

The feeling of wrongness was stronger here. This wasn't unusual in itself. Many places Oliver visited when questioning people with Langham felt this way—just not as strong. Or as sinister.

"This is one nasty-arsed case," he mumbled.

"And the others we've worked on weren't?" Langham cut the engine and slipped off his seat belt.

"They were, but this one... I don't know. It's hard to explain."

"Then don't. Soak it all up, see what you get when we go in, and tell me once we've left. I'll do the talking. You just concentrate on picking shit up."

Langham got out of the car, and Oliver did the same, his stomach heavy with dread. He hated this part of investigations. Negative energy always found him, and he saw sights and heard sounds no one should. Terrible things, horrible noises. Voices.

After walking up the paved path bordered by a well-kept garden with a recently mown lawn and pruned hedges, they stood on a shiny, red-brick step.

Langham glanced at Oliver and knocked. "Got anything yet?"

"You know, the usual. Something being odd, knowing we're going to find out some shit we hadn't expected."

"Right." Langham knocked again. "Good."

They waited a minute.

"Wonder if he's out?" Langham walked across to the large window beside the door, presumably the living room. "If he *is* out, he needs to tidy up when he gets home. Looks like someone's had an unfriendly visit."

Oliver moved to stand beside him and peered through the glass. "Are we going in?"

"Yep. Could be a man in distress inside, know what I mean?" He went back to the front door, aimed a few hard kicks, bursting it open. "I'll go first. Stay behind me."

Oliver followed Langham inside, immediately hit by the stench of blood. He heaved, breathed through his mouth in a small hallway littered with coats flung down from the hooks on the wall just inside the doorway. Someone had been here, and he didn't need the growing unease in his gut to tell him that. He stepped over the coats, tailing Langham into the living room. The mess here was worse—sofa overturned, the wall cabinet pulled down and balancing precariously on an armchair, contents strewn over a carpet covered in fluff from inside the throw cushions. One mental fucker had been looking for something, all right.

Langham turned, cocking his head to let Oliver know they'd find nothing here but chaos. In the kitchen, there was more of the same wreckage there, then they went upstairs. Langham coughed, gagged, and stopped at the top, glancing across the landing at the two closed doors. Oliver stared at them through the baluster rails, a wave of hate flowing over him. The press of spirits wanting to speak to him sent him breathless. He swallowed, knowing there was nothing to fear here with regards to another human being. No one was at home.

No living person anyway.

"Someone's dead in there, probably Reynolds," he said.

Langham turned to look down at him. "Yeah, the smell's unmistakeable, but I told myself maybe he had a dog that had died or something. Ever the optimist, me."

"He's in that room." Oliver pointed to the door closest to Langham. A snapshot of what lay behind it flashed through his mind. "And it isn't pretty. You might want to take a few deep breaths. He's, um, he's a fucking mess." He swallowed bile, shaking his head to remove the image, though why he bothered when he'd see it for real any second now he didn't know. Habit.

"Right. Bloody wonderful." Langham walked towards the door, taking a tissue from his pocket to turn the handle. "Get ready to be hit in the face by the smell."

Oliver covered his nose and mouth. Langham opened the door, and, expecting the stench to override anything else, Oliver was shocked to find it was the last thing he needed to think about. Blood soaked the walls, near-black now it had dried, arcs and splashes, rivulets and streams that spoke of a violent death. The bed was soaked with it, the quilt hardened with the stuff, and the carpet was ebony in small, circular patches where the victim had possibly staggered around the room, falling every so often as his life had ebbed away.

But there was no corpse.

"What the fuck?" Oliver said, his frown hurting. "I saw him. Saw the man all cut up. He was on the bed. Faceup. Eyes open. Arms hacked off."

"Well, he isn't here now." Langham stepped back—right onto Oliver's toe.

"Shit! You might want to watch where you're stepping."

"It would help if you weren't right up my arse."

Then it struck Oliver. The press of spirits wasn't plural. It was one. Reynolds. It had to be. "Um, I'm going to let him in."

Langham spun to face him. "You got Reynolds on at you?"

"I think so."

"Then what are you waiting for?"

Oliver sighed and unlatched the locked door inside his mind. The spirit came tumbling in, as if he'd been leaning against it with all his might, and Oliver *felt* the spirit's disorientation as it fought to regain its equilibrium. Heavy breathing filled

Oliver's head, and the sense of a panicked man covered him in a heavy sweat.

"Calm down," he said. "Take a moment before you speak."

Oliver waited, staring at Langham. The detective's face showed how impatient he was for information, but this was Oliver's domain, and he called the shots here. The breathing lightened, was less ragged, and a low humming came, like an abused kid trying to drown out the sound of his parents fighting.

"It's all right. Just take your time. We're not going anywhere. And we're here to help catch who did this to you. I know it's difficult. Know how painful this is. How much hard work it is. But just focus on what you need to tell me, and if you can give me images, too, then that would be great."

The humming stopped, leaving only the sound of breathing—from all three of them.

"Eyes like madness. Couldn't get over them, the way they flickered like that. Didn't used to be that way. Can't get to grips with it. Didn't like it. He's been tested on, like those kids. He wasn't like he was before... He said...he..."

"It's okay. Slow down. Start at the beginning. Don't tell me about your death, either, tell me about him. Concentrate only on him."

This bloke was going to burn out his connection if he wasn't careful, then Oliver and Langham would be left with fuck all new to go on. He quickly shielded his thoughts from Reynolds while he awaited his next outburst. It wouldn't do for him to feel under pressure.

A huge sigh filled Oliver's mind, then—

"Yes, he's been given that stuff I found out about. Been experimented on. He's like a super-human. Great strength."

Another sigh.

"He had a woman's wig on. Some kind of mask or makeup. So he knows, knows he's doing wrong—otherwise, he wouldn't wear a disguise. He knows right from wrong. He was brought up properly."

"You're doing well, Mark. Keep going."

Langham squeezed past Oliver and went to stand on the landing.

"I ripped his wig off when he... I pulled out some of his real hair. Saw that on TV once. They said if you were attacked to try and rip out some hair, scratch skin so it went under your nails, give the police something to go on. I did that. I was right, wasn't I? Right to do that? Even though it was him... Maybe I shouldn't have tried ratting him out like that."

"Yes, Mark. Excellent. Where are you?"

"I'm here with you."

"No, where is your body?"

"He took me out of here. Put me in a van."

"Think about the van. What colour is it?"

"It was red. Dark red. Small, like a car without back seats. He's had it for a while. I remember when he showed it to me before..."

"Go on."

"He took me to this field. Muttered something about some bitch being dumped up the way a bit. I didn't know who he meant, but I'm guessing I wasn't his first. Didn't think he'd come for me. Not him. Never thought he'd be like that."

"Who? It's like you know him."

Silence.

"Was there a river nearby, Mark?"

"Yes. I'm... My body's on a bend of the river. It's... I'm half in the water, half out. Like, my hands are in the water."

"Fuck."

"What? What did I say wrong?"

"Nothing. It's fine. Keep going." Oliver thought of the water doing its damage, possibly taking away those hairs, that skin beneath Mark's nails. The killer knew exactly what Mark had been up to.

"He said, 'There. A little bit of sweetness for you.' Then he sprinkled some of those things on me. You know the kind I mean?"

"What things?"

"That stuff you get on cakes. Sprinkles over icing."

"Sugar strands?"

"Yes, that's it. He said Gran used to pour them into his mouth when he'd been bad. Said they filled his mouth so he had trouble breathing. And she wouldn't let him spit them out. He had to sit there until they melted. He said he wouldn't make me eat them, just sprinkled them on me so everyone would know I'd been bad. But he's lying. Gran never did that. And he told me it was ironic the medication

48

was in the same form. Like those strands were haunting him."

"You didn't do anything wrong, Mark, except to try and make this right."

"I did do wrong. I poked into something I shouldn't have. Found out what they were doing. I'd been in his room before that woman at work showed me the notes. He'll come for you next because he knows you know. You and him over there. Be careful. He comes quietly—he's right there before you even know it. And he slices and cuts, stabs and chases you around until you can't get away anymore. Until..."

Mark's breathing intensified, his panic returning.

"Now, think about that van. Did you catch any of the number plate? Anything about it that might help us?"

"No. But I know where he lives. I know him."

"You do?" Jesus, why hadn't he fucking said so from the start?

"Because I forgot."

"You weren't meant to hear that, Mark. I'm sorry."

"Right. You want to know where he lives, who he is?"

"We do." Oliver held his breath.

"He lives in the basement of this old house."

"Tell me where."

"It's in Saltwater Street. That old thing on the corner. The one with the dirty windows with filthy net curtains. Gran lives there."

49

"Your gran?"

"Yes. She's still there. Old as the hills but there just the same."

"And his name?"

Mark sighed. *"Bloody easy to answer that one. He's my brother. Alex Reynolds."*

CHAPTER SIX

Oliver staggered against the banister as Mark disappeared. Quickly, to save Langham battering him with queries, he related the information.

"So," Oliver said when he'd finished, "do we have the same situation with Alex as we have with PrivoLabs? Only a dead man's word on Alex's guilt so we can't barge in and arrest him?"

"Something like that, but we *can* go and ask him if he knows where his brother is. Make it look like we're after Mark, not Alex. He might slip up."

Oliver shivered. "Yeah, or he might well do to us what he did to Louise and Mark. This bloke sounds like he's been programmed to prevent people finding anything out about what Privo are up to. Except we've got a good idea—and really, we ought to think about telling Shields about this shit, just in case something happens to us and the information we have dies with us."

Langham walked down the stairs. "Yeah, but if we tell him... You know what he's like. He'll poke his nose in, break the case, and take all the credit."

"Rather that than us being dead," Oliver muttered, following him. Outside on the path, he asked, "You calling this in?"

Langham nosed about in the garden, looking for God knew what. "Yep, so Shields will hear about it anyway."

"Exactly. So go directly to him, saves you repeating yourself, because you know he'll want the ins and outs of the cat's arsehole if he hears the news from someone other than you. He can deal with this place while we go over to Alex's— and you *are* going to tell Shields where we're going, aren't you?"

"Yeah, yeah, stop fucking nagging."

"Sod you."

Oliver turned away, leaving Langham to call Shields. Oliver faced the cottage and closed his eyes. Maybe, if he concentrated, Mark would come back, or Louise. They'd given him excellent information, but he couldn't shake the feeling that this wasn't going to be a cut-and-dried case. Okay, Louise had given Mark the notes, and Mark had investigated, finding out a load of info he hadn't expected. Louise had been killed over what she knew, Mark for the same reason, but how the hell did someone kill their own brother like that? Had Alex been changed so much by the drugs that he'd lost the knowledge that Mark *was* his brother? Was he forced to kill *anyone* who got in PrivoLabs' way? Alex must have been one fucked-up bastard before Privo had got hold of him. If the tale about the gran and those sugar strands was true, that man had serious issues he needed to deal with. They were spilling over into his kills, which meant the experiments hadn't succeeded in taking away every part of him, the basic essence of who he'd been before.

So what was the point in PrivoLabs' experiment? To allow people to seem relatively normal until someone needed killing? To have them act as they would prior to the experiments, and some switch or whatever was flicked, turning the human lab rats into nutters who went about doing abhorrent things? The owner of Privo was one sick git.

Oliver turned to face Langham.

"Come on, we've got to wait for someone to turn up here, then we're going to Saltwater Street." Langham strode towards his car and got in.

53

Oliver stared for a moment in shock. Langham usually made some caustic remark about Shields when he'd spoken to him. Something had pissed him off for him to just walk away like that.

In the car, Oliver asked, "What's up?"

Langham started the engine, letting it idle while he stared ahead and flexed his jaw.

"You okay?" Oliver kept his gaze on Langham.

"I will be in a minute. Just got to digest what that prick said."

Oliver remained silent, unwilling to press. When Langham acted like this, it was best to leave him be—he'd come around in his own time. After several minutes sitting in silence, though, Oliver grew antsy for an answer. The distant wail of a police siren prevented him prompting Langham again, and he sat with his mouth firmly closed until the coppers arrived to secure the scene.

Langham spoke to them through his window then sped off towards the city. Still silent. Oliver rubbed a spot on his jeans as though they were dirty.

He couldn't take this any longer. "Okay, so what did Shields say?"

"I mentioned Alex Reynolds, and he said he'd wanted to talk to me about him. Said the guy had called in earlier as a concerned citizen and told them I'm a bent copper. Said Alex thought that wasn't right. Has Alex been watching me since this started? Since he followed you as you left Louise's death site?" He slapped the steering wheel. "That's what the wanker's done. He's been keeping tabs

54

on us. Shields said Alex had given him your number plate, lied and said he'd seen me talking to some shifty 'gangsters' outside PrivoLabs."

"That's bullshit. We got straight in the car after we'd been there and drove off."

"I know that, but Shields doesn't. And let's face it, he'd believe anything bad someone said about me. You especially."

"That arsehole can find a cliff and jump the fuck off it."

They journeyed in silence after that, Oliver thinking on why Langham had got so upset over what Shields had said. If he wasn't bent, what was the issue, or did coppers get arsey about shit like that?

In no time at all, they were driving down Saltwater Street, and the heavy feeling of foreboding made itself known inside Oliver. He tensed—it seemed every muscle in his body hardened. Taking a deep breath, he glanced across at Langham, who frowned at the dilapidated building Mark had described.

"Looks like no one's lived there for years, although there's a light on." Langham parked.

Oliver stared at the house. It was similar to the pub in the hamlet, all wonky walls and concave roof, and he was surprised it still stood, what with the state it was in. It must have been here for over a century—the façade showed serious signs of wear and tear, and the brickwork was rough, not as uniform as the more recently built houses around it. He sighed, trying to shake off the air of oppression in the car, and moved to get out.

Langham grimaced. "If Shields does something about what he's been told, stirs trouble when I haven't done anything wrong... No bastard's pissing about with my life. I'll have it out with that Shields wanker later, but for now, we have work to do. We've got to focus, because if Alex is in there and he turns nasty?" He paused, then, "We should have backup, really."

"But we're only asking him where his brother is. We can feel him out and return with uniforms later."

"Yeah, but didn't Mark say his brother had turned nasty in a second? That he'd crept up on him or whatever?"

Oliver nodded. "There's two of us. We can question the old lady if you think it would look better, make Alex think we're not there for him in any way. Let's just see how it goes, and if he goes for us, we'll deal with it then."

Langham fumbled with his seat belt, cutting the engine once he'd freed himself. "Fucking mental becoming a copper. Dad always said that. Too much of a risk. Unpredictable people. Yet here I am, walking into something that could be the end of me, taking a civilian in with me. Maybe you ought to stay—"

"I am *not* staying in the car. We go in together. Besides, you might need me. I might pick up on something in there."

Langham sighed. "It's useless arguing with you."

With both of them out on the pavement, Oliver said, "Come on. Let's get this over and done with."

They walked, heads down, along the path made of broken patio slabs, the cement between crumbling, gone in places. Oliver got a dose of trepidation—it filled him, growing from his toes right to the top of his head, a cold, spiteful fear that left him shaking.

"Something's off here as well."

Langham reached the front door first. "Like what? Tell me."

"Like at Mark's place. I don't think Alex is even here." That piece of knowledge eased Oliver's mind somewhat, but the fact that something was going on inside those walls still bothered him. "It isn't clear what's happening, but we're going to find more than we bargained for."

"All right. Calm down and concentrate. I'll knock."

Oliver nodded. Langham lifted a tight fist and banged on the door. No one answered, and they waited for a moment, then Langham knocked again.

"Fucking déjà vu," Langham said, rapping a third time. He walked to the window, another living room Oliver would bet, and held his hands over his eyes to peer inside. "No angry visitors in this one, but the old woman's asleep. She's got something on her nose, but I can't make it out."

Oliver hammered the door—hard and insistent.

"No movement from her," Langham said.

"Probable cause to kick the door down?"

"Yep. I could have thought she was dead."

Oliver nodded, and Langham walked back to the door. It took several kicks to the wood for it to give in and admit them. Langham went first, as always, and rounded the doorframe to their right, entering the living room the elderly lady was in. Caught up in the adrenaline rush of going inside a house without permission or a warrant, Oliver didn't catch the sense of a new death. Not until he stood in the centre of the room behind Langham, whose wide frame blocked Oliver's view of the old woman. He peered around him and recoiled at the sight. She sat on the sofa, head against the back, her mouth filled with those sugar strands, nose held closed with a clothes peg.

Alex was one sick bastard.

"Jesus," Langham breathed, pulling out his phone and calling in her death.

Oliver reversed to the doorway, wanting to put distance between himself and her. He didn't think he could take her spirit latching on to him and spilling the last moments of her life. In the hallway, he waited for Langham to join him, and, with gloves on, they followed their usual pattern of scouring the lower and upper rooms before coming back down to stop at a door positioned under the stairs.

"Mark said his brother lived down in the basement, yes?" Langham asked.

"Yep. But he isn't there. I'd say he fucked off once he killed the old woman. But we'd better check anyway."

58

Langham opened the only door they hadn't tried. Oliver sighed. Something evil was down there. Langham switched on the light, revealing surprisingly clean plastered walls that turned left at an angle halfway down. Oliver steeled himself to face whatever it was waiting for them and followed the detective down steps that creaked every time they trod on them. The sense of dread grew stronger as they rounded the corner, the light from the stairway giving scant illumination, highlighting only the floor directly before them. The basement could be small or large for all Oliver knew—the blackness beyond that slice of light hid absolutely everything—and he felt along the wall for another light switch. He brushed his fingers over the protruding plastic square and flicked it on.

Sound exploded, like frightened jungle birds, all caws and startled shrieks. Oliver jumped, squinting in the burst of light to try to get used to the brightness.

"Oh, fuck me sideways," Langham said, moving forward at speed.

Oliver stared ahead at several cages holding children whose ages ranged from about four through to eight. "Oh my God. I wasn't expecting... I didn't know... Shit!" He walked towards them, smiling to put them at ease, but they continued squawking, their pitch rising, as did their volume. "It's all right. Everything's going to be all right."

Langham fussed with a padlock, trying unsuccessfully to get it open. The children had retreated to the backs of their cages, looking stunned and frightened to death. What the hell were they doing here? Had Alex been hiding them for PrivoLabs? What kind of outfit *were* they, to not have them at least kept secure in a proper environment? Not that keeping them locked up like this was right, but fuck, in a basement? In cages?

A rapid-fire shift of movement caught Oliver's eye, and the kid inside the cage Langham was working on darted forward.

"Langham! Watch it!"

That child's pupils were black slits in a circle of lurid blue. Langham jumped back just before the kid crashed against the cage door, mouth open, teeth gnashing where the detective's hands had so recently been on the padlock.

Langham stepped back, eyes wide. "He was going to *bite* me!"

Oliver's heart hammered, and his legs went weak. They needed to get out of here—and now. Something else was about to go down if they didn't leave this place. Them being here had clearly upset the kids. Who knew, if they were angry enough, whether they could break out of those cages and attack. He wasn't sure what urged him to grab Langham's sleeve and propel them up the stairs, but he wasn't about to hang around to analyse it.

CHAPTER SEVEN

Shields and other coppers had shown up within minutes of Langham making the call. The big, greasy bastard strolled towards them, a smug smile filling his fleshy face as though he thought them a pair of wimps for not remaining in the basement.

"So there are kids down there then?" Shields raised his hands and waggled his fingers. "Oooh, kids that fly at you with intent to bite. Nasty business, that. I'll have to go down there and give them a good telling off."

"Be my fucking guest," Langham snarled, striding towards his car. He shouted back, "And if they chew your fingers off, don't say I didn't warn you."

He got in his car. Oliver joined him. Langham sped up Saltwater Street, and Oliver refused to think about what could be happening to Shields.

"Where do we go now?" he asked, looking at Langham. "Are you okay?"

"I will be once I forget about Shields. He isn't worth wasting thinking time on, but you know what it's like. He gets under your skin."

"He does. I wonder if they've bitten him yet."

"Probably."

"He'll be cursing us. That you warned him and he didn't listen."

"Good. A bit of humility won't hurt him."

"I take it we're going to Privo?"

"Yep."

"To do what?"

"Talk to the manager, the owner, whatever. Tell him we heard rumours, see what he has to say, check out his reaction."

"But wouldn't that be alerting him? Letting him know we're on to him?"

"It'll be all over the news shortly. No way those kids being found can be contained. Someone will leak it to the press. Better we go to Privo before the owner sees the news and gets his story straight before we speak to him."

Oliver absently rubbed the bandage keeping his broken finger strapped to the one beside it. It ached.

"My brother came for lunch."

"Pardon?" Oliver said, unsure whether he'd heard the voice in his head right.

Langham sighed. "I said—"

"No, I wasn't talking to you."

"Right. Okay, I'll keep quiet." Langham gripped the wheel tighter.

Oliver prayed Mark hadn't just managed to make a connection with one sentence that told him jack shit. He closed his eyes and waited.

"Alex came to lunch where I work. I'm—I was an accountant. That's why... Louise, that's her name... That's why Louise was filing, why she found the notes. They were in PrivoLabs' papers. She showed them to me, and I rang Privo, let them know we had something that didn't belong in their account file."

"And?"

"I went back to work and did a bit of digging. Asked this lab technician I know at Privo to keep an eye out, see what was going on. Told him what was on the note. He said it was about a new drug he'd been testing. That it wasn't ready yet. Next day, some bloke I hadn't seen before, from Privo, turned up when I was eating lunch in the courtyard outside my work with Alex. The bloke, he said he needed the note, and I gave it to him—had it in my inside pocket, didn't I. Anyway, after he'd gone, Alex started asking questions. I told him what the note had said, what the lab man said, and..."

63

"And what?"

"He wanted to blackmail them. Said he'd make some money out of them. That he'd threaten to go to the papers. So after he left, I went back inside and rang the lab technician again, but..."

"But what? Mark? Mark? Shit. You still there? Tell me what happened then?"

"I guess they got to Alex. Fed him those meds."

"Yeah, that much is pretty obvious. Who's the technician?"

"Ronan Dougherty, lives in the flats above the corner shop on Kater Road, but I can't—couldn't— get hold of him. His phone rang off the hook."

"Fuck."

"I think—"

"Yep, me, too."

"Alex..."

"Yep, he's probably paid the tech a visit already."

"He wasn't like that before. Not mean like he is now."

Oliver shielded his thoughts. If Alex was willing to resort to blackmail, he wasn't your average kind of bloke. Anyone who could hatch a plan pretty quick like that and go off to make it happen... Yeah, Alex was a bad lot, no matter what Mark thought—the drugs had just made him worse. Privo had him under their control, offing everyone who knew about what they were doing. It was only a matter of time before Alex got to him and Langham.

"Anything else?" he asked Mark.

Silence.

"Mark?" Oliver waited.

No response.

"Well?" Langham demanded.

"We're next on the list. Got to be. We know about Privo, therefore, Alex has to kill us. After we've been to Privo, we need to go back to Louise's field. Mark's body is still there, remember?"

Langham handed Oliver his phone. "Shit. Sorry to do this to you, but ask for Shields. If he can't come to the phone, we know he's been bitten."

Oliver stifled a smirk. "So I'm telling him, or whoever, where Mark is?"

"Yeah, you need to lie, make out you've only just been told by the dead. If they find out about the time lapse and that we already knew Mark's location, I'm fucked."

Oliver made the call and was put through to Shields, who never mentioned the kids and said he'd head over to the field now and asked that Langham report to him once they'd been to Privo.

Oliver put the phone in the cup holder and asked Langham, "Why did Shields ask that you report to him? He's not above you in command, is he, so...?"

"Like I said, he wants people in his pocket. He knows I'll know exactly what he means by telling me to report to him. It's a game. If he tells the chief I'm bent, even though I'm not, someone will look into it—I'm to let him call the shots so he doesn't do that. Come on, we're here. Time to question whoever's in charge of this fucked-up place."

In Privo's reception, Oliver expected to feel some familiarity, but he didn't. The plants had gone—some soil was still scattered around the base of the pots—and one sofa was missing.

The receptionist looked at them with fear in her eyes, and her mouth worked like she wanted to tell them something but struggled to get the words out. "C-can I help you?"

"We need to speak with the person in charge here."

"Mr Jackson isn't available at the moment. We had a..." She stared ahead at the space where the sofa had been. "An unhappy visitor an hour ago, so Mr Jackson is...indisposed."

"Indisposed in what way?" Langham produced his ID. "Is he ill? Not here?"

"No, he's here, but he said—"

"I don't care what he said. I need to speak to him."

The receptionist widened her eyes at Langham's tone and maintained eye contact as she reached out for the phone. She dialled without glancing at the keypad and jumped when someone answered. "S-sorry. Yes, I know you said... There are detectives here." She eyed them keenly. "Yes, that's them... Oh, right. Well, I'll send them up then."

Oliver's stomach muscles tautened. If the push inside his brain was anything to go by, spirits were trying to warn him that something wasn't right.

"Mr Jackson will see you now," she said, pasting on a fake smile. "Use the lift. Top floor, the only office up there."

"Thank you." Langham strode towards the double silver doors of the lift. He jabbed the button and tapped his foot.

Oliver joined him, whispering, "He knows."

"Yep." Langham flexed his jaw.

"How are we going to play this?"

"Don't speak—make out you know what I'm talking about once we're in the lift. He could be listening, so I need to spout bollocks." Langham stepped inside and glanced up into the top corner.

Oliver followed him and his gaze. A camera studied them.

"Right," Langham said, clearing his throat. "We'll alert Mr Jackson about the ridiculous rumours circulating about his company, then we'll go to that corner shop where we got those microwave curries from before, you know where I mean?"

Oliver got the gist—the lab tech's flat—and nodded. "Yep, been a long day. I'm starving. Pick up some beer, too."

"Sounds good." Langham sighed. "I hate having to bring this kind of information to someone. The potential those rumours have to ruin a company doesn't bear thinking about. Malicious, that's what people are."

"Too right."

The lift came to a perfect, gliding stop, and the doors slid open. A huge space met them, an open-plan office that took up the whole floor. Several desks were dotted about, but only one was occupied. It was situated rear centre, shielded from the others either side by black zigzag screens. A man sat behind the desk, head bent, giving them the impression he was hard at work and had nothing to hide, thank you very much.

Langham cleared his throat again, and the man looked up.

"Mr Jackson?" Langham asked.

Jackson stood, rounding his desk and strolling towards them with the air of someone who was at ease with who he was. His dark-grey suit—pressed so well that his trousers still bore the strict line down the front despite the fact that he'd possibly been sitting for untold hours—fitted him just right. No pulling material on broad shoulders here, or a tight waistband. Shoulder-length wavy hair, that strange colour between brown and black, Antonio Banderas in his eighties days.

"Ah, hello, Detectives," Jackson said.

Langham didn't correct him.

"What can I do for you?" Jackson walked towards his desk, looking back over his shoulder with eyebrows raised as though asking if they wanted to follow him.

They did, and once they were all seated, Langham said, "I'm sorry to bother you with this, but we thought it best we told you personally. Rumours are circulating about your company doing experiments on children—and on a man named Alex Reynolds. Of course, this is utterly

68

ridiculous, but we felt you should know in case something unfortunate hits the news later tonight."

Jackson sat straighter, covering his slip of alarm by making out he was reaching for a pen and notebook. He held them in hands that didn't shake, held their gazes, too, an unwavering stare that spoke of him being calm and collected now.

Clever bastard.

"Really? How on earth did you come by this information?"

Langham rolled his eyes. "Some children were found in the basement at Alex Reynolds' home. If he's to be believed, your company has been conducting experiments on them."

"Experiments on children? That's a little far-fetched, don't you think?" Jackson did the flabbergasted look well.

"Indeed," Langham said. "Between you and me, we think Reynolds is trying to hide the fact he had the children down there for...*other* reasons."

"Oh God. That's disgusting." Jackson put his pen and pad down.

"People will do anything to get themselves out of trouble, sir, but we wanted you aware. If it leaks out what he's said... I don't have to tell you the devastating effects this could have on your company. Even if he's lying, people will remember the PrivoLab name for all the wrong reasons."

"Well, thank you for coming to tell me. I'll alert my staff and let them know we have a 'no comment' policy should they be approached by the press."

"Very sensible." Langham paused. "So, you wouldn't object if we asked to take a look around? Specifically at your labs?"

"Of course not. I'll take you on a tour immediately."

"Very good, sir. I can phone my chief once we've had a nose about and tell him the rumours are totally unfounded—he's expecting us to call him in half an hour or so. Hopefully, if we're quick, I can get that information to him before the news airs. Perhaps he'll be able to telephone the newsroom and let them know he's available for comment. It can only help your company."

Jackson stood quickly. "Yes, yes. I'll show you around right now."

CHAPTER EIGHT

"**W**ell, that was a waste of time," Oliver grumbled.

They sat in the car in the delivery area out the back of PrivoLabs.

A massive bush, which had protested with a groan of branches and the spiteful scratch of thorns on car paintwork as Langham had reversed into it, shielded them from view. Of course, Jackson could have seen them hiding the car in his shrubbery, but then again, he may well have been too intent on covering his arse to have bothered peering out of the window at whether they'd driven away or not. Maybe Langham's ruse about the rumours had worked, put Jackson at ease. Perhaps the bloke had believed him.

"I'm not qualified to know what the fuck we were looking for," Oliver went on, "and any drugs they had on the shelves appeared to be the same as any I can get over the counter in the supermarket. And you do realise he's going to dump any drugs relating to those kids now, don't you?"

"He won't. They cost too much. Shit, these leaves are seriously thick. I can't see much except the back door of the place. He'll call someone, you'll see." Langham leant forward and squinted to see through the foliage. "They'll come and collect the drugs and anything related to them."

"And I take it we'll follow."

"Yeah."

"So what about visiting Ronan Dougherty's flat? Seeing if he's been cut up, has arms missing like Mark? See if those strands are all over him?"

"Shit!" Langham whacked the steering wheel, narrowly missing blasting the horn. "What the hell is wrong with me? I forgot about him. Call it in to Shields, same deal as before—you've only just been told by the spirits. Tell him what we're doing, too."

Oliver did that, wincing at the sound of Shields' smarmy voice coming at him over the airwaves.

72

"I told you to tell *Langham* to report to me," Shields barked. "Not you. What's he doing that has him so tied up he can't speak to me?"

"He's the one who'll be driving, following the people, if they come to collect the drugs." Oliver closed his eyes, willing himself not to snap back, but his mouth worked before he could stop it. "Why, did you want to taunt him about being a bent copper again, is that it?"

"Fuck off, you spirit-hearing little bastard."

"Ah, so you admit I *do* hear them then? That it isn't *me* killing these people?"

Shields spluttered. "No, no, that's not it at all. I still think it's you. That you have a gang, some blokes who kill when you're with Langham so it just *looks* like it isn't you."

"Oh, give me a fucking break, shithead."

Langham lifted his eyebrows at that, smiled, then continued studying ahead.

"Shithead? I'll have the chief take you off civilian duty for that. You shouldn't even be with Langham now. You've probably had a quick chat to the drug-makers in those bushes, haven't you. Langham going to sell them on, is he?"

"Knob off. I'll speak to the chief about the crap you come out with. The way you treat me."

Shields laughed, hard and rough. "Prove it. Just let me know if something goes down."

Oliver ended the call.

Langham quickly glanced at him then back at the Privo building. "Jesus, I knew you were a

73

mouthy little sod, but I didn't think you had it in you to bite back at Shields."

"He's pissed me off for long enough."

"Fuck, someone's here. Hand me the camera, quick."

Oliver fumbled in the glove box and pulled the digital out. He switched it on. "Battery's low."

"I always forget to charge the bloody thing. Thanks."

A large white truck backed into the Privo yard, reverse alarm bleeping. Once it had stopped, four men dressed head to toe in black poured out of the cab and approached the back door. It opened, and Jackson appeared in the doorway, head darting left to right as he inspected the area. Obviously deeming it safe, he ushered the men inside and closed the door.

"You catch all that?" Oliver asked.

"Yep. Got some good close-ups, too. Keep your eye on the door. Let me know when they come out again. I'm just going to check the pictures I took." He glanced down at them then switched the camera off. He reached for his radio. "I'm going to need backup."

He relayed that unmarked cars needed to be at the rear of Privo for when Langham and Oliver followed the truck once it left. Whether that meant those coppers would go in and arrest Mr Jackson, or wait to follow him in case *he* left, Oliver didn't know. He had no time to contemplate further either—the black-clad men were coming out, loading boxes into the truck.

"Langham…"

He looked up. "So he does have something to hide. Bastard." He took more pictures.

Oliver lost count of the boxes once they went over fifty. That was some serious amount of drugs there. Maybe the shit they'd used to make them, too. Everything was evidence these days. Oliver imagined Jackson panicking, wondering how the hell he could cover his bases, ensuring that those workers oblivious to what he'd really been doing with those drugs still only thought they'd been working on something innocent. Who knew, maybe he'd just announce he'd pulled the plug on their research, that the drug wasn't viable, too expensive to produce, something like that. Whatever he did, he'd have to do it fast. Just by Langham snapping pictures of him had him bang to rights for *some* kind of crime. Aiding and abetting. Whatever. So long as the man went down for a stretch and the killings stopped, Oliver would be happy.

"Hold up," Langham said. "They're on the move." He barked into his radio that backup ought to get here pretty damn quick.

The truck rumbled to life, Jackson standing at the back door. The vehicle eased forward and nosed out onto the main road. Then Jackson closed the door, the truck joined the light traffic, and Langham took the opportunity to start his car and follow. The branches had a jolly old time of it scratching the paintwork again.

There were only two cars between Langham's and the truck, and they tailed it at an acceptable thirty miles per hour. No bringing attention to themselves. No smartarse overtaking to get closer. The truck was large enough to be seen for a good few hundred yards ahead, so providing they remained on this straight road for a while, they didn't risk losing it.

The two cars turned right, stalling Langham and Oliver for a few seconds. Oliver's heart rate increased, adrenaline speeding through him too fast for comfort. He felt sick, had never been on a pursuit before, and had no idea what Langham had in mind. Would they just follow until the vehicle had reached its destination? If they did, didn't they risk being spotted if the end of their journey was in some remote place?

"What's next?" he asked.

The truck had turned left onto the slip road leading to the motorway.

"We follow, see where it goes."

"So we don't flag it down, get them to stop?"

"Not at the moment, no. There are too many men inside for me to deal with should they get nasty. Got to wait for that silent radio to squawk and let me know *we're* being followed by other coppers. I could pull them over on a random check, ask to look inside, and then what? If we find those sugar strands, yep, we'd have reason to take the men in, but like I said, one of me, four of them. They're not likely to go with me without a fight. Looked a nasty set of bastards, didn't they."

Oliver agreed. Big, burly men they wouldn't stand a chance against. "It's obvious they've got the drugs in the back."

"Of course they have. Forensics will have a field day finding out what those strands contain. Wonder if they've got around to doing those from Louise's body yet?" He snorted. "Doubt it. They're way behind with evidence processing. Always are. You'd think there'd be more employed for times like this, when we need a quick analysis in order to bring someone in. We need solid proof the strands on Louise and in that old woman's mouth are the same ones in the truck. And those they'll find on Mark's body."

"Wonder if Shields has arrived there yet. And I wonder what they're going to do with those kids. How they'll get them out without being bitten or attacked."

"Only thing I can think of is sedating them, and that doesn't sit well with me, seeing as they're drugged up to the fucking eyeballs already. Poor little bastards."

Oliver thought of their parents, frantic with worry for however long their children had been missing. Of the police, busy now matching each child to every missing person report. Visiting those parents. Breaking the news that their previously cute kid had possibly killed. "This is such a mess."

"It is. Bet you wish you didn't hear voices now, don't you."

Oliver nodded. He didn't need to answer verbally. Didn't want to. If he did, everything he felt inside would tumble out. Like how he'd coped with this all his life, borne the ridicule of his family for being such a 'weirdo'. Did they see him in the newspapers, on the news, as the same weirdo? Or did they now wish they'd been more understanding? He was famous around here, kind of. People knew his face, stopped him sometimes, shouted insults at others. He just wanted to live a quiet life, but fate had had other things in mind from the day he'd been born.

He gusted out a breath full of resignation. He was stuck as he was whether he liked it or not. Couldn't ignore the voices any more than he could choose not to breathe. It just wasn't happening.

"You okay?" Langham glanced over with a look of concern.

"Yeah, was just thinking."

"Of?"

"The past. Now. The future."

"In what way?"

The truck took another slip road, one that rose to join an overpass.

"Me, being the way I am. Wishing I wasn't. Wishing I was normal."

"And my question brought that up for you. Sorry."

"It's okay. Nothing I don't think about by myself from time to time anyway. I mean, it's hardly something you can ignore, is it. I could go to some channeller, get them to teach me to tune the dead out, but I'd only beat myself up over who the spirits would turn to after."

"Catch twenty-two."

"Yep."

"Look." Langham pointed. "The truck's heading towards Lingbrough."

Oliver peered ahead. "If they stop there, unload somewhere, it wouldn't surprise me. Quiet village. Houses few and far between. Not the type of place to be spotted by a nosy community. I heard that place has snobs living there. No one wanting to be friendly with anyone else."

"Perfect hideout."

"Yeah." Oliver glanced back to see if they were being followed. They were, by a beat-up, old-style Ford Escort van, a nineties job that looked as though it'd be better off on the scrap heap. A *red* van. His guts bunched. "Your undercover backup tend to drive red rustbuckets?"

"No." Langham stared in the rearview mirror for a second. "Fuck. Reckon that's Alex Reynolds?"

"Who the fuck knows. This is the first time I've been involved directly with one of your cases so I don't know how this works. Find the body, report to you, and go home, that's me. I don't get to see all this bullshit usually. Mark said Alex owns a red van. Jackson might have called him to tail the truck."

"Just thought the same myself. If Alex has been watching us like I think he has, he'd have already clocked my car way before now. So Jackson will also know what we're up to. Fucking great."

Oliver looked back again. "No sign of any other cars behind the van either."

Langham snatched up the radio, asking where the fuck backup was. He was told three miles behind. "Well, they ought to put their foot down on the pedal then, because we've got Alex Reynolds on our tail." He hooked the radio back on the dash. "I don't fancy him behind doing the same to us as he did to you when you found Louise. Wouldn't put it past him either."

Mark Reynolds had said Alex hadn't acted like he usually did. Those drugs had a lot to answer for. As did the man who'd ordered them to be made and distributed with intent to make people kill. Jackson. What an arsewipe. Another thought hit Oliver then. Maybe Jackson was just a middle man, the one with the means to create the drugs. What if someone else had approached *him* with the drugging idea? Someone with a shitload of power who wasn't to be ignored if you knew what was good for you?

This was way bigger than he'd imagined, and being here now in the thick of it didn't seem such a good idea. Yet he'd insisted he was tagging along with Langham to every lead. For some reason, this case had got to him more than the others—maybe because Louise had contacted him *while* she'd been being killed and not after.

He didn't get to ponder that further. Alex pulled alongside them.

And rammed his van into the side of Langham's car.

"Not again," Oliver said, leaning forward to stare out of Langham's side window at Alex. "This bloke is *mental.*"

"There are a lot of them about." Langham held tight to the wheel to keep the vehicle on the road. He glanced sideways, then gunned the accelerator, gaining a car-length's space between their back and his front. "And they don't tend to give up easily."

Langham's statement was proved true with a shunt to the rear of his car. Oliver pitched forward, flung his hands out to brace himself on the dash. His broken finger throbbed at the contact.

"If that bastard breaks another of my fingers, or something else of mine, I'll kill the fucker."

"By the looks of things, he's going to give it a good go." Langham drove faster, almost catching up to the truck. "I'd better move, in case the truck is ordered to stop and we go up its arse, Alex going up ours. I don't fancy being inside a concertina sandwich, do you?"

"Not really, no."

Oliver closed his eyes, praying this would all end soon—with good results. Relief poured into him at the sound of sirens, and he stared through the back window. Help had arrived. Other officers had finally got their arses into gear and put some speed into their pursuit. Four unmarked vehicles followed, one overtaking Alex to slip between Langham's car and his, two boxing him in either side, and one at the rear.

"So now what?" Oliver hoped backup would also take care of the truck.

"We carry on following *them*," Langham said.

Shit.

CHAPTER NINE

L angham wedged his car behind some high-
as-a-house bushes, one of the backup
vehicles beside them. As they sat observing a large
house situated in expansive grounds down a lane
just off the motorway, awaiting further backup,
Oliver took a moment to calm down. News had
come via one of the officers in the next car that
Alex Reynolds had been apprehended, a clawing,

insane mass of anger that had taken six officers to subdue.

He took the binoculars Langham handed to him.

"You have a turn. My eyes are crossing."

Oliver peered through them. The truck was parked directly outside the house, a sprawling monstrosity that spoke of high maintenance and a shedload of cash. The men weren't about, no doubt inside, secreting the drugs and whatever else they'd removed from Privo. The coppers en route were trained to get inside and round the inhabitants up, secure the truck and its contents, and Oliver thanked fuck for that.

Langham's mobile rang, startling Oliver so the binoculars banged his brow bone. He lowered them and glanced at the caller display. Shields. Langham jabbed the speakerphone button.

"Yep?" Langham closed his eyes for a second, probably steeling himself for whatever the other detective had to say.

"Langham?"

"Who else?"

"Wasn't sure if your *friend* there would be answering. You still outside the house?"

"Yep."

"The team not arrived yet?"

"Obviously not, otherwise I wouldn't be here."

"As soon as they do, I need you back here."

"What for? Can't you cope with Ronan Dougherty's flat and Mark Reynolds' site by yourself?" Langham smirked.

"Not amusing. That's sorted. Dougherty's dead, as you suspected. Arms hacked off, face slashed. Mark Reynolds. Dead. In the field like your weirdo said. Officers are dealing with it all now."

"So? What do you want?"

"Like I said. You. Back here."

Oliver experienced all kinds of irritation, so God knew what Langham felt—he was the DI, for fuck's sake. Langham clenched his teeth and drummed his fingers on his thigh.

"Paperwork?" Langham asked.

"You wish," Shields said, his oily tone grating yet slick at the same time. "No, we've got another couple of bodies. Different to the others."

"So there's someone else out there. Unless Alex offed them before he followed us, changed the way he does things to throw us off."

"He's too up himself to do that," Shields said. "He'd have wanted us to know it was him, that he was one step ahead. In control. No, this is an amateur. A bloody messy one at that. And I know who the hell we're looking for, too."

Oliver suspected Shields wanted Langham to beg for the answer. Wanted them both to know he was in the lead now, the one dishing out orders.

"Right," Langham said. "Won't be long. The team will be here in a minute. It'll take us about twenty to get back. Where do you need us?"

"Us? No, I need *you.*"

Langham sighed. "Oliver comes with me."

"That's disgusting."

"Very funny, Shields, but that's your filthy mind talking. You know what I meant."

"Right. I need you at fifty-four Bridgewater Road, back in the city. Soon as you can. You have to see this scene to believe it. It'll give you an idea of just what we're dealing with."

"'What'? Don't you mean 'who'?"

"Well, yeah. Can't have been right in the head before she took the drugs."

"She? Jesus…"

"Yeah, she. A four-foot, pigtailed blonde."

"You've seen her? Know her?"

"Yep, I've seen her. She's one of those kids from Alex's basement. Gave an officer the slip just before they made it to the police van that'd take them to hospital. Feisty little bitch, too."

"This just keeps getting better."

"Yeah, well. Nothing we can do but find her before she kills someone else. And when you get here, you'll see how much she enjoys it an' all."

Oliver stood beside Langham on the pavement outside fifty-four Bridgewater Road. A sense of desolation took over him. This wasn't your average home. Just seeing the state of it told him that. Snot-smeared windows, where kids had been staring outside, or maybe they had a dog who relished slobbering on glass. A front door with red peeling paint, the letterbox rust-spotted, the numbers five and four wonky beside it. Unkempt garden, abundant with weeds and household debris—a TV with a smashed screen and a chest of drawers with the handles missing. A supermarket shopping trolley, too.

Jesus Christ.

He imagined the homes either side would lean away from their companion if they weren't part of a terrace. The stench wafting out of the open front door was enough to put anyone off entering. Age-old shit and urine, over-cooked cabbage, raw meat, all combined into an aroma that almost had Oliver gagging. And this was winter. He couldn't even imagine the smell in high summer.

Shields barrelled towards them in protective clothing, out of the house and down the cracked concrete path, a white handkerchief pressed to his nose. Oliver took a minute to enjoy the man's obvious distress.

"Oh Jesus," Shields said, blinking rapidly and stuffing the hanky in his suit pocket. "That *house*..." He shuddered, swallowed, his Adam's apple bobbing. "Like no one *ever* cleaned."

"Tell me what you know. About the girl," Langham said.

"Abused kid, by all accounts. Neighbours say she wasn't looked after properly. Didn't need them to tell me that. Stayed up all hours, left alone most of the time while the parents were out on the piss. And when they were home they were pissed then, too. Damn shame. Neighbours hadn't even been aware she was missing, just assumed she'd been kept off school like she had in the past, not allowed out, that kind of thing."

87

Shields took in a large breath, his facial expression showing he fully expected the air to be rank. When it wasn't—or evidently not as bad as it was inside—he smiled with relief.

"Parents report her missing?" A tic flickered beneath Langham's eye.

"No. Apparently, the girl—"

"She have a name?"

"Yes, Glenn Close. Can you believe that? She turned into a bunny boiler just like her namesake, too."

Oliver wondered how Shields could joke like that. Yeah, he knew coppers had to, in order to get through the day, the horrific things they dealt with, but Oliver's heart had been twisted with the knowledge that drugs had made this little girl commit murder. That her life had been one of neglect and without love prior to her taking those drugs, only for her to be catapulted into a different kind of horror. Poor kid.

"Go on," Langham urged, clearly impatient. He tapped his foot, ran a rigid hand through his hair.

"So, if the neighbours are to be believed, Glenn—still can't get over that name—had run away before. Returned after a day or two. Maybe her parents assumed this time was the same."

"Maybe they didn't care," Oliver said.

Shields ignored him. "So, that's her background. No other family except those in that house. No friends. And no one knows where she went when she did go missing. Social Services were aware of her, but you know their policy—best to keep the child with her mother for as long as they can, even if that mother's off her face half the time."

"Heard about that myself," Oliver said. "The wrench of separation is apparently far worse for the kid than placing her in a nice home where someone gives a shit. Makes no sense to me. Children can adapt. She'd have got over it, had a better life. Now?" He couldn't finish what he'd wanted to say. The thought of where Glenn would end up should she be caught didn't bear thinking about. A damaged soul forever, most likely, always thinking she was in the wrong, that no one cared.

Shields stared at him like he'd spoken out of turn, and also like Oliver was a piece of shit he was only tolerating. He turned away, looked at Langham. "So, when you go inside, you'll understand the mess you'll see."

In booties and with gloves on, taken from a cardboard box nearby, they followed Shields up the path. Ordinarily, Oliver would have entertained shoving the man forward so he tripped, and he laughed to himself about the imagery, but he was fucked if he could do that now. Emotions gripped him—those of whoever had been killed inside—and they weren't pretty.

"Fucking little bitch. Knew I shouldn't have had her. Was going to get an abortion, wasn't I? But my old man reckoned it'd be a laugh to have a kid. Social Security payments would go up. So I had her, and look where it got us."

89

Oliver stopped walking, held his hand up to alert Langham that the dead had spoken. "Where is she?"

"Don't know, don't fucking care."

Langham stopped, too, waving at Shields to do the same. The smarmy detective gave an eye roll and huffed out an impatient breath. But he halted.

"You don't have any idea where she might have gone?" Oliver asked.

"No. Well, maybe. Made a pal for herself with some old biddy down the road. Reckon that's where she fucked off to when she disappeared for days on end. Pissed me off, that did. I had no one here to make my cuppas."

Oliver bit down on his tongue. He wanted to rip this woman a new arsehole. Her cackling laugh, rich with phlegm, churned his stomach.

"Down this road?"

"Yeah. Number ninety-seven. Mrs Roosay, some poncy name like that."

Oliver couldn't hold his anger back any longer. "And it didn't *bother* you? You just let your child go there without checking the woman out *first?*"

"Course I fucking didn't. Why would I? Got her out from under my feet, didn't it?"

He couldn't resist his retort. "But your cuppas..."

"Yeah, there was that, but I wasn't too fussed, not really. Wouldn't have been long before someone else would be there to do it."

"What do you mean?"

"Nosy bastard, aren't you?"

She cackled again, the sound fading.

He pinched the bridge of his nose, a headache threatening to lay him out. "She's gone. Didn't offer much except the fact that Glenn visited with an old lady at number ninety-seven. A Mrs Roosay."

Shields lifted onto his tiptoes, peering down the street. "That's along there. Come inside here first, Langham, then you can take your lapdog down there and interview the neighbour." He shook his head. "I knocked on that door, too. Thought she was out."

Oliver was too weary to snipe back about the lapdog comment. His energy had been sapped by Glenn's mother, leaving behind the taint of evil and utter disregard for anyone but herself. He sighed as they stepped into the house, signed a scene log, and he mentally prepared himself for what he was about to see. He hoped to God that woman wouldn't contact him again once he stood by her body.

"In here." Shields led them through a doorway in the hall and into a lounge. He stood in the centre, looking to his left, and out came the handkerchief again.

Langham joined him, and by the expression on his face, Oliver wasn't sure he wanted to follow. Langham had paled, his lips were drawn back in a grimace, and the frown that appeared gouged deep crevices.

Oliver went in.

Glenn's mother was an unrecognisable heap of innards, legs and arms protruding from it.

Intestines, heart, lungs, kidneys, and her liver mounded high inside a ripped-open stomach that had bled profusely. The air had dried them out a little, darkened them, but the carnage wasn't something you could imagine. It had to be seen to be believed.

"Where's her head?" Oliver whispered.

"Over here," Shields said, the words muffled by his hanky.

Oliver followed Shields' pointed finger. The head sat in the corner, wedged on top of a pile of scrunched-up newspaper and oily fish-and-chip wrappers. An upended fast-food cup lay beside it, and there was a note next to that.

"What's that say?" Oliver asked.

"Kid's writing, bit of an angry scrawl but legible," Shields said. "It says: *Here's your fucking tea*. I assume the cup had tea in it, judging by the darker stain on the carpet around the neck stump, but it's difficult to tell, what with the amount of blood."

Oliver allowed himself a small smile at the sense of victory Glenn must have felt then. He didn't condone killing of any kind, but in this situation... No, he wasn't going to go there.

"There's something else, too." Shields gestured to the opposite corner. "Another note as well."

Oliver dared himself to turn his head. What appeared to be a foetus lay curled in the corner, a filthy, ragged blanket over it, only the head poking out.

"And *that* note?" Langham asked.

Shields moved to the door behind Oliver. "Says: *I saved you from doing it.*"

Oliver pushed past Shields and went out into the hallway, his mind swimming with what Glenn must have put up with for her to have killed her mother knowing she was pregnant. Her logic in killing her unborn sibling wasn't lost on him. She'd saved the child from a life of hell like she'd had. Christ, she must have suffered, harboured so much rage, and the drugs had given her the impetus to erase it all. Except it would be in her mind, lingering. Always. He understood why it was such a rage killing. Drugged and crazed Glenn might be, but somewhere inside was a little girl who just wanted to be loved and accepted.

Sickening. All of it.

"There's another one." Shields walked past Oliver, making a show of ensuring they didn't touch in the small space, and walked upstairs.

Langham followed, his expression grim, taking the stairs one at a time, arms by his sides, as though every ounce of energy had been sucked out of him. Oliver felt the same, and when he trailed the two detectives, his legs felt like they'd give way any minute and he'd tumble back down, landing in the filth of the hallway, stinky old shoes and a broken tennis racquet for a pillow.

On the landing, one strewn with dirty washing, bursting black bags—he was surprised this household even owned any or knew what they were—and an odd assortment of bric-a-brac, he breathed in through his mouth. The whole house was filled with the stench of death, cloying and thick.

Inside the box bedroom, a man sat on a bare mattress stained by his blood and who only knew what else. Dark stains, light stains—piss and shit most likely—and patches of crusty dirt that may well have been mud or food. He wasn't sure and didn't much want to entertain it further. The body held his gaze then. Sitting up like that, he looked for all the world like a normal bloke, just taking a nap in the nude. His eyes were closed, his hands clasped over his beach ball belly, and his black hair flopped forward over one eye. Both legs stuck out in front of him, the backs of his knees touching the mattress edge, the heels of his feet on a matted fluffy rug.

But he no longer owned a penis. It sat beside him, holding down a note, an obscene paperweight. Blood had dripped from it, leaving a dribble that had meandered across the page, a now black-encrusted river.

She'd cut it off when he'd been alive then.

But how had she killed him? Nothing else appeared out of place.

"This note says: *Hope you enjoyed your dinner*," Shields said. "Seems obvious the girl had cooked for them, been a skivvy. She must have fed him something. Won't know what that was until the ME's had a good look at him and the tox screens come back."

Langham cleared his throat. "That penis. Indicates she did more for him than cook dinner."

"Seems that way." Shields walked out, calling from the landing, "Mrs Roosay. Number ninety-seven!" as though *he'd* been the one to get the tip and they'd known nothing about it until he'd just said.

Oliver wanted to find Glenn so those drugs were taken from her system and she was given some understanding somewhere. How old was she? Depending on that, she might be tried as an adult and sent away. He didn't think that was fair. She deserved help, a better life, a family who gave a monkeys.

That she possibly wasn't going to get it had Oliver belting out of the room and down the stairs, back out onto the broken concrete path Glenn had trudged up and down all her life, leaving and entering a home where no one cared if she existed—except for the fact that she made cups of tea, cooked meals, and gave her father more than he had a right to take.

CHAPTER TEN

Mrs Roosay turned out to be Mrs Rosé, a French woman of indeterminate years. She stood on her doorstep, back hunched, shoulders rounded, and squinted at them through thick-lensed glasses. Her home-knitted cardigan, brown with hints of beige running through it, crossed over at the front, her arms clamping them to her.

Out of the protective clothing, Oliver felt less official.

"Glenn, you say?" she asked.

"Yes." Langham smiled. "Have you seen her today. Or recently?"

Oliver studied her. She didn't display body language that spoke of her hiding information. Or holding a child in her home. She seemed weary, tired deep in her bones, and bewildered that a detective stood on her front path asking about a little girl.

"I have not seen her for weeks. I have been worried, but there is nothing I can do. The authorities, they do not listen to me. Say it is 'all in hand'. I do not believe them. How can it be all in hand if the child is still dirty and uncared for?" Tears filled her eyes.

"Did you allow Glenn into your home at any time, Mrs Rosé?" Langham's voice was soft, kind.

She nodded. "I would rather tell you inside. Please, come."

Mrs Rosé led the way into her living room, the house the same layout as Glenn's. Except this one was clean and well cared for. Family photographs covered the walls and every available surface— end tables, the mantel, the television—and the air smelt of furniture polish and fresh washing. Glenn must have loved it here and wondered how her home could be so different.

Oliver and Langham sat at Mrs Rosé's gesture to do so, on an overstuffed sofa covered in pink chintz. She settled in a matching chair to their right and gazed out of the front window with rheumy eyes.

"She is a dear thing. I waited for her. To come here and visit. But she did not come. The last time she was here was my birthday." She looked at Langham, her smile sad and watery.

"When was that, Mrs Rosé?" he asked.

"Two months ago. August seventeenth. She said she had made me a card, that she would bring it…" Her lower lip quivered.

"And the time before that?" Langham prodded.

"Every week on a Saturday morning. I have missed her. I wondered if the authorities had finally listened to me and taken her away, because I saw her getting into someone's car. That car had been outside the house before, and the child had spoken to whoever was in there. Through the window."

She'd grabbed Oliver's attention with that.

Langham sat up straighter, then leant forward to take the old woman's hand in his. "Can you remember what day that was?"

She nodded. "A Friday. The Friday after she had been here on the Saturday." She frowned, as though the date eluded her. "I cannot remember…"

"I can work the date out, Mrs Rosé, don't worry about that." Langham gave her a gentle smile. "The car. Can you remember it?"

She nodded. "Very expensive. Black. With one of those badges on the front. A Mercedes. The man who collected her did not enter her house. I had been pruning in the front garden and saw Glenn pass. She did not see me. Her head was down, as usual. But she glanced up just before she got to the car. The man got out and folded his arms on the roof just above his open door. He smiled, talked to her, but I cannot tell you what it was about, I could not hear. Glenn nodded, and he reached inside the car. He handed her something. Perhaps a cake, I am not sure, but she ate it there on the path."

A cake...

Mrs Rosé raised one hand to her heart and closed her eyes. "Then the man walked around the front of the car and opened the passenger side. Glenn nodded, smiled up at him, and it seemed she knew him because she got in. Then he drove away, and I have not seen her since." She stared at Langham. "I should have telephoned the police. But I thought... The car had been before..."

Langham patted her hand. "It's fine, Mrs Rosé. Please don't worry or blame yourself. You've been a great help. This may be a long shot, but did you happen to notice the number plate?"

She smiled and pulled her hand from his. Stood on rickety legs and shivered over to the mantel. "Now *that* I can help you with. I had seen the car so often, but that was not the reason I remembered the plate. I wrote it down but have not forgotten it." She took a slip of paper from behind one of the photographs and handed it to Langham.

Oliver leant across to read it. In her spidery handwriting, Mrs Rosé had given them shocking information. It was a personal plate. A name. One

Oliver hadn't expected to see. It had to be a mistake. Was that man capable of abducting a child? It went against the grain, all he stood for—unless he'd turned into a bent copper himself recently. Langham had paled significantly.

5H13LD5.

He wasn't imagining it, was he? Wanting to see something that would bring that smarmy wanker down?

Langham cleared his throat. "Thank you, Mrs Rosé, you've been more help than you can imagine."

"Will you... Will you come back and tell me when you find her?" The old woman smoothed her skirt then patted her hair. "I have grown to love her."

"Of course," Langham said. "And if I don't call round, I'll telephone, all right?"

She nodded, then wrote down her phone number. After handing it to Langham, she showed them to the door on unsteady legs, fingers fluttering beside her.

They stepped outside, the front door closing behind them with a soft snick, and Oliver inhaled a deep breath. He had so many questions battering around inside his mind. A headache wouldn't be long in coming. The lack of sleep was getting to him—he was all liquid bones and weary muscles—but his brain, it buzzed. He walked to the end of the path and turned. Langham still stood by the front door, finger and thumb toying with his lips as he stared at the carefully cut grass.

It reminded Oliver of when he'd stared at the office carpet.

Langham lowered his hand. "It can't be him, can it?" He looked up, frown firmly in place, mouth a hard laceration. "I mean, he's a copper. So fucking righteous. So *correct* all the bloody time."

"People change," Oliver said. "Who knows what the lure of money does. If he's involved, that is. If that's the way this is panning out."

Langham nodded, gaze back on the ground, although he walked towards Oliver and met him on the pavement. "You reckon he has it in him to be involved? To be on some psycho's payroll? Taking a kid, for fuck's sake?"

Oliver swallowed. "I'd like to say no. That the way he carries on tells us he's well into law enforcement, wouldn't be involved in anything dodgy. But honestly? He's a bastard—I've always said that. An out-and-out bastard. With that personality? He's capable of anything, if you ask me."

Langham nodded again. "Shit. So what do I do? Ask him? Watch him? Tell the chief?"

"No idea. Not my call. For what it's worth—my opinion—I say we have him watched, see where he goes, what he does."

"Have him watched? That means letting someone else in on this. Trusting someone not to tell him."

"What about running that plate? Might not even be his, just us jumping the gun."

"Yep. Come on."

Oliver trailed him down the street, back towards Glenn's. Shields was outside, a posturing peacock, invisible tail feathers splayed as though he'd caught some woman on his sexual radar. But no woman was around. He was alone, strutting up and down the path, mobile to his ear.

Langham held his arm out, stopping Oliver mid-stride. He tugged him closer to a hedge high enough to hide behind and not be seen. Close enough to hear. "Listen…"

"It's not like that," Shields said. "Well, that's what I'm about to do, go and find her. That's my job… No, I didn't expect for her to escape—no one did… Like I *meant* for this to happen? Muddy the waters? Christ, the last thing I want is my job complicated. Bad enough we had Alex going around killing people, let alone her."

Who was he speaking to? It could be an innocent conversation, but that number plate coming to light had shed a new slant on what Shields was saying. He could be talking to Jackson at Privo…

"It might be innocent," Oliver whispered. "We might be hearing what we want to hear."

Langham gritted his teeth. "Shh."

Shields coughed lightly, then, "Langham? He's interviewing a neighbour. What? Am I worried about that? Why should I be?"

Oliver's guts bunched. *Innocent conversation? Is whoever is on the other end of that line reminding him his car might have been clocked in this street?*

102

Shields laughed, strutted up and down some more. "Fuck, no. I'll give Mrs Roosay a visit once Langham's gone. Check what he said to her. Whether she saw anything."

That had sounded sinister, like Shields would be warning Mrs Rosé off.

"Right," Shields said. "We'll have this one dealt with in no time."

Oliver couldn't stand it any longer. He walked forward, out into the open, making his way towards Shields. The detective had his back to him, his greasy hair shining despite the pale, feeble sunlight. On Glenn's path, a crisp packet crinkled under Oliver's tread.

Shields spun around, eyes narrowed, his eyebrows quivering. "Yes, I hear you, sir. Will do." He stared harder at Oliver. "Where's Langham?"

"Here," Langham said, his voice gruff, barely concealed emotion sneakily bristling out of him.

"Any news from the Roosay woman?"

"No," Langham said quickly. Too quickly. "She's just some old French woman." He shrugged and shook his head. "So now we need to regroup, work out what we've done so far, who's dealing with what, and where we go from here."

Was it Oliver's imagination, or did Shields sigh with relief just then?

"Right." Shields whipped out a notebook. "Go for it."

Langham said, "Louise is at the morgue, her scene still being searched. Mark Reynolds, I presume, is in the same place, his scene being inspected. The old woman, Reynolds' gran. What's the status on that?"

"She's with Louise and Mark." Shields jotted on his pad.

"And Ronan Dougherty?"

"Last I heard he was still in situ."

Oliver studied Shields while the man's head was bent. He looked for signs of discomfort, of guilt, but found none. Either he was one clever bastard at disguising how he felt, acting innocent, or he had nothing to do with this.

"And then there's these two." Langham wrote in his own pad. "Three, including the foetus. You dealing with them?"

He'll say yes, because then he can visit Mrs Rosé. Can't see him taking Langham's word for it that the old bird doesn't know anything. Shit.

"May as well, seeing as I was first on the scene." He smirked, like Langham being out of the loop at that house with the truck in the middle of nowhere made him a lesser detective. "I'll also put things in motion to find Glenn." He chuckled. "Glenn Close. Jesus..."

Arsehole.

"Fine," Langham said. "The truck men are being dealt with—must get an update on how that's going. Any news on Jackson?"

"He's being watched until the warrant comes through to search Privo," Shields said.

The man appeared affronted, as if Langham questioning him wasn't right. As if having to answer to him didn't sit well. Of course it wouldn't,

Shields being Shields, but Oliver saw him through new eyes now. Wanted to find the buried nugget that proved he was in on this shit. He shook his head, thinking of the times Shields had accused him of having a hand in the murders Oliver had brought to their attention, when all along he was—*possibly*—involved in bollocks like that himself.

"So we're up to date," Langham said. "I'll call in, see if there are any tox results back yet. Yep, I've got high hopes on that, but I want to know what the hell's in those sugar strands that makes a person act like this." Langham gestured to the house, arm raised, then let it slap back down to his side. "This has turned into a fucking nightmare."

Shields turned away, muttered, "And it'll only get worse."

"What was that?" Langham said.

Oliver's instincts screamed that Shields was guilty, but he shushed the roaming thoughts—the words sliding through his mind sounded too much like his own voice, not those of the dead. He couldn't trust it.

"Let's pray it doesn't get worse," Shields said, louder this time, then disappeared inside the house, that damn hanky covering his nose and mouth.

That's not what you said the first time.

"Come on." Langham strode towards his car, stiff-limbed, anger seeping out of him. He raked a hand through his hair, tightened it into a fist, and jerked open the driver's-side door with a more-than-annoyed tug.

Oliver trotted to keep up then climbed inside.

Langham started the car. "If it isn't him, if he isn't involved, I'll eat my fucking badge."

"He said 'sir'. Could have been talking to the chief."

Langham let the engine idle, taking his phone out of his inside jacket pocket. Stared at Mrs Rosé's phone number. Jabbed in the digits. "Mrs Rosé? Ah, hello again. It's Detective Langham. I was at your house a short while ago. No, we haven't found her. I'm calling on a different matter." He glanced at Oliver, his face grim. "If another detective calls at your door, don't answer. In fact, if anyone you don't know knocks, ignore them. For now. Until I get back to you. Why? It's better that you deal with me, seeing as I spoke with you. I'll send someone out to keep an eye on you." He waited a beat, then said goodbye, dropping his phone back into his pocket. "That's her safe and sorted. Now, I think we need to visit Ronan Dougherty's place, see him for ourselves, unless he's been moved since Shields last got an update." He clamped the steering wheel. "Fuck. The dodgy number plate. Must remember to run that through the computer."

CHAPTER ELEVEN

Ronan Dougherty looked disgusting. No other word for it. Not only had his arms been hacked off, but he'd been eviscerated, his insides outside, much like Glenn's mother. They sat in a pile on his stomach, the skin pulled back like a half-peeled orange, forgotten by the person who had wanted to eat it. Blood coated the beige carpet beneath him, a living room carpet that, everywhere else, was clean and well cared for.

Ronan's place was tidy—a man who liked order, cleanliness—the surfaces recently polished, now marred by arcs of blood spatter that spoke of a frenzied knife attack. The way the red stuff had landed on the walls and ceiling indicated it was castoff, droplets flying off a knife before the blade had been plunged back into the body.

Alex had been angry here, unable to contain it, had stabbed and stabbed, possibly long after Ronan had died. Those drugs, God, they changed a human into a monster.

In his protective outfit, Langham sighed. "I've seen angry kills before, but this is something else. Think of Louise. Imagine what she'd have looked like if you hadn't turned up. Yep, Alex went back, finished what he'd started, but her body wasn't like this one. This resembles Glenn's parents. It's like Alex and Glenn killed Ronan together."

"Maybe they escalate with each kill." Oliver cocked his head, waiting for Ronan to make contact. He wasn't sure if he could take that now, if he could listen to what the poor man had to say. He was tired. So fucking tired. "Maybe the drugs make them worse the longer they take them. Higher doses or whatever. Could produce differing results from the same killer."

Langham stepped forward, then crouched beside the body. "The strands are here. Most definitely Alex's work."

Oliver stepped from foot to foot, his booties and white suit rustling. No way was he getting any closer to that body. Like Louise the second time around, Ronan had no face. His scalp had been treated like an orange, too, yanked back to expose a bloody, rounded dome of skull with a harsh, jagged divot in it.

"Blunt force trauma," Langham said. " Rectangular weapon. A gun handle?"

"But if Alex had a gun and just wanted to kill to stop Ronan speaking out, why not just shoot him?"

"Because the drugs make him want to kill in a frenzy, to obliterate the victim bearing any resemblance to a human being. I'm guessing, by the way, but that makes sense to me. Feels like I'm on the right track. If you just want to kill someone, to keep their mouth shut, you generally don't see this kind of rage. Rage means emotion, a connection, that it's personal."

"So Alex took it personally that Louise and Ronan had made moves to expose him and the Privo shit, is that it?"

"Who knows?" Langham stood, stared down at the body. "He was messed up well before the drugs by the sound of it. Those strands, his gran— can't have been a healthy upbringing, *if* he's to be believed. The old dear might not have done any of it, like Mark said."

Oliver thought about the similarities between himself, Alex, and Glenn. He could so easily have been them. Mean adults, being taunted by them all his life, not fitting in anywhere. But he hadn't turned out bad, and who knew, maybe Alex and Glenn wouldn't have if they hadn't been force-fed drugs. Force-fed. Sounded more like they'd taken them willingly, so he couldn't even blame that on whoever had given the strands to them.

Of course they'd have taken them willingly. Who wouldn't mind eating a doughnut like that if one was offered? Who'd suspect the strands on top would contain something that would change their lives forever?

Not Oliver. He'd have accepted it like he'd accept a biscuit with his cup of tea. Not Alex, who may well have been given one when he'd gone to blackmail Jackson. And not Glenn, who'd been probably so starved of not only love but confections, that she'd gobbled it down eagerly.

Like Langham had said, this was a fucking nightmare.

The medical examiner's men loitered, waiting for Langham's nod before they went about their business, removing the body and taking it to a place where the secrets hidden from the casual observer would be revealed. They had one hell of a job on their hands today, the amount of bodies turning up in the state they were. Murders weren't unheard of here, but the volume, all at one time, was.

Oliver moved out of the way, standing close to the wall beside the door as Ronan's body was taken out, prone on a stretcher, the sight of him covered by a sheet from prying eyes.

What a shitty way to die.

"It is, isn't it?"

Oliver tensed. "Is that you?" He flapped one hand at Langham.

"Me? Yes, this is me." The man chortled. *"Didn't expect to see myself being carried out like that, but there you go. Life's full of surprises."*

Oliver smiled at Ronan's upbeat tone. "You sound all right about it."

"Well, there's nothing I can bloody do about it now, is there? No point pissing and moaning about something I can't change. May as well get on with my lot and be done with it."

"Good way of dealing with it, I suppose. Do you have something you want to tell me?"

"Damn right I do. That's what I'm here for, isn't it, a bit of gossip and all that?"

Oliver would have liked Ronan in life. "What can you tell me? What do you remember?"

"Well, after I started sticking my nose in where it clearly wasn't wanted"—another chuckle—*"I found out something a bit surprising. I mean, it all points to it being Jackson, doesn't it? I thought the same, but the man hasn't got any fucking idea what's going on right under his nose."*

Oliver frowned. "But that doesn't make sense. After we visited Privo—"

"Yep, I know. I tagged along for the ride there. He was getting rid of some other stuff. Been making drugs for a rival company, hasn't he, the dirty bastard. He doesn't own Privo, just runs the place. The owner leaves it to him, no questions asked, just rakes in the cash, thanks very much."

"So he was removing other drugs? Totally unrelated to the strands?"

"Yep. Shitting himself, he is. Funny to watch. Anyway, the owner would be a bit pissed off about Jackson making money on the side, so Jackson's covering his arse by removing them."

"Does the owner have anything to do with the strands and what's going on there?"

"Fuck, yes. She's in on it."

"She?"

"Yep, and you wouldn't think it to look at her either. Not mentioning any names and all that, but some of us dead folks who've spoken to you haven't been telling the truth. Put it this way, they haven't lied, they just haven't told you everything. Maybe they're in denial, who knows?"

Oliver thought on who'd contacted him. Louise. Glenn's mother. Mark Reynolds. "Who?"

"Ah, I wouldn't like to say. It'd take the fun out of your investigation, wouldn't it?"

"But by you not saying, you're hampering it."

"So what do the police do when they don't have someone like you, who has someone like me filtering them information? They investigate, that's what."

Ronan's voice faded.

"Come on now, Ronan. That isn't fair. This isn't a game. You can't leave it hanging like this. Just give me a name. I can't contact spirits—they have to contact me—so it's not like I can burst into their death sleep or whatever and demand answers."

"Louise."

It came softly, a whisper of sound Oliver barely caught.

"You need to look into Louise."

112

"Into? As in, literally inside her body?"

Ronan didn't answer. His presence had gone, leaving Oliver battling a wave of fatigue.

"What did you get?" Langham asked, his face full of concern.

"Give me a second." Oliver held up his hand. "I'm knackered." He shook his head, willing some life back into his aching limbs. His broken finger throbbed so hard he had the urge to yank it off.

"Come on, into the car."

Oliver followed Langham outside, leaving the other detectives to it. They took off their togs and, inside the vehicle, Oliver rested his head on the seat, eyes closing. It felt like he hadn't slept in days, like the first call from Louise had been months ago. He berated himself for not asking Ronan about Shields being involved, but the conversation had taken on a life of its own.

Langham drove away, and Oliver kept his eyes shut until the car stopped again. He looked around—nothing but a dingy street, the walls of aged houses either side, the bricks uneven, knobbles and gouges spoiling them. Langham had parked, sandwiching the car between two others, and with no pedestrians in sight, it felt as though they were the only people on the planet.

"Talk to me." Langham said.

"That was Ronan."

"I gathered that. And?"

Oliver turned his head towards Langham. "He said someone lied to me. That we had to look into

Louise. Whether he means inside her body or into her life, I don't know."

"Louise? Did she give you the impression she was lying?"

"No, she sounded genuine enough, but now I think about it, she was hesitant. And she didn't give the right information. Remember? We thought she'd worked at Privo. She'd implied that. And she'd mentioned a 'she'. I took it that she wasn't too happy about her son being with her mother, but what if she meant someone else?"

"Family feuds, happen all the time."

"So what d'you reckon Ronan was on about?" Oliver sighed out the words.

"Louise has probably got something on her body, some evidence, something that will help us. If being dead is like I imagine it to be, you can float about all over the damn place and find out information. He's probably done that. Whatever, it all helps—any information helps."

"There's a lot we need to do. Coppers all over the place, all dealing with different victims. What started out as a case between me and Shields has expanded. Possibly too many chefs in the kitchen, but what can we do?"

Oliver didn't know. "And shit, I forgot to say. Jackson isn't in on it."

Langham frowned. "You're kidding me. That man looked guilty as fuck."

"He *is* guilty, but not of drugging Alex and those kids. He's working for the competition, using Privo

114

as a place to mass produce drugs for them. That was what he was getting rid of."

"If we'd known that before... What a waste of time and resources. Give me a sec." He grabbed the radio, asking for, then being connected to the detective dealing with the Jackson side of things. "Yeah, you got Jackson at the station now? Okay, is he talking? Ah, right. A lot of denial. That's because he doesn't know what you're talking about. Ask him questions leading to an answer on whether he's making a quick quid on the side. See if he grabs the chance to admit to that—it's got to be better for him than taking the blame for this other shit. Yeah, right. That's what I thought." He relayed what Oliver had told him. "Okay? So go with that. Thanks."

"A massive can of worms." Oliver sighed.

"It is. I need my bed."

Oliver needed his, too. Speaking to so many dead people in one day had taken its toll. Zapped the energy out of him. He could just close his eyes now... "Too much to do, though," he slurred, giving in and allowing his eyes to shut.

"Yep. We need to run that Mercedes plate. Need to find out who owns Privo. Need to deal with Louise." Langham sounded as weary as Oliver felt. "So, after we do that, we go to the morgue."

"What?"

"You heard me. You need to get your feet wet there sometime. We have to see Louise. And you wanted it this way, wanted in on everything this time."

Oliver had—did—but the thought of seeing Louise in such a sterile place, tools poking into places they had no right to be, had his guts rolling over. "Right. Yeah."

He remained silent as Langham drove them back to the station. They strode inside and went into Langham's office. He sat at his desk, tapping the keys and moving the mouse. Threw himself into his chair, which scooted backwards a bit, banging into a metal filing cabinet behind.

"It isn't Shields," Langham said. "Yet I could have sworn it was."

"Who is it, then?"

"A woman, same surname. Cordelia. Fifty-four. Lives in that big house up by the river. You know the one?"

Yeah, Oliver knew it. Reminded him of a mansion every time he saw it, with those white walls and fake Greek columns holding up a veranda that skirted halfway up the property and all around. He'd often wondered who lived there, and now he knew, although the name didn't ring any bells.

Langham grimaced. "So now we need to know why a man was driving Cordelia's car, why he visited Glenn, and why the fuck he took that little girl away."

Oliver nodded. The day was pushing into evening. Time was pressing if they wanted to visit Louise then Cordelia Shields. "Morgue first?"

"Yeah, morgue first. I'm beginning to think this day will never end."

"Me, too."

CHAPTER TWELVE

The overhead lights gleamed onto the metal table holding Louise's remains, the glare bright enough to hurt Oliver's eyes. To actually be here, with different scents combating for dominance—the tart stench of disinfectant, the whiff of dead bodies, his fresh sweat—gave him a sense of disembodiment, like he viewed it on a screen, wasn't *really* there with a room along the corridor holding drawer upon drawer of corpses.

Who the fuck would *choose* this as a profession? Who would want those smells inside their noses even after they went home, those odours seeping deep into their skin so they were never free of them despite bathing? He wanted a shower so badly, so God knew what the ME felt like. Maybe he was used to it. Maybe even *liked* it.

That ME, a kind-eyed, black-haired, rotund man of about forty, tended to Louise with such care and respect that Oliver changed his mind about him and his job. Someone had to do it.

Langham introduced him to Oliver as Hank, and Oliver would have shaken his hand in any other circumstance, but the bloodied latex gloves ensured he kept his arms by his sides.

"I've sent the sugar strands and hairs—fortunately for us some have the root still attached—to forensics. Others, well, they're not real. I'd say they're synthetic," Hank said.

Langham nodded, stepped closer to the table. "Yes, the bloke wore a wig. We know who he is anyway, but the confirmation will only strengthen our case."

"Ah, always the last to know these things, me." Hank smiled and continued his perusal of Louise's insides. "Nasty business, this. And there's more bodies here, waiting in their silent way for me to find out what they have to say despite being dead." He nodded over at three more tables, bodies covered with white sheets. "My assistant needs to get his arse into gear and put them in the fridge.

What's he doing? Was only supposed to have gone for a piddle."

Oliver had wondered why they weren't refrigerated while Hank worked on Louise.

"All related murders, I'm told." Hank walked to a shiny whiteboard on the wall beside the door. "A Mark Reynolds, Geraldine Reynolds, and Ronan Dougherty here as well as Louise. So, this is a serial, yes?" He moved back over to Louise, peeling back what was left of the skin on her face.

Fuck me...

Langham said, "You'll have more bodies in shortly. Male and female. Although they're related in the case to these poor bastards, they weren't killed by the same person. If you'll believe it, a young girl killed them."

Hank shot his head up, stared at Langham with his mouth wide open. "What, a young girl killed these people here?"

"No, sorry, I wasn't being clear. A man killed these four, but the girl killed the other two you've got coming in. There's also a foetus. When you see the female victim, you'll wonder how a four-foot kid had the strength to do what she did, but she had the help of drugs."

"Oh my. Well..." Hank picked up an electric blade. "That sounds most disturbing. The youth of today, eh? Any road, is there anything I can help you with, because I need to...you know...off with her head!" He slashed at the air with his blade, his red cheeks shining with sweat.

Oliver's knees buckled.

Hank laughed. "Not literally, dear boy. Just cutting the top off. Need to have a wee look at her brain."

Bile surged up Oliver's throat and settled on the back of his tongue. Good job he hadn't eaten lately.

"We just needed to have a nose inside Louise here, unless you can tell us what we need to know. Not that we even know what we're looking for," Langham said. "Inside her torso. Did you find anything there other than the strands and the hairs?"

"A bit of fibre, nothing to tell the neighbours about," Hank said. "Apart from the fact she was hacked more after death than when she was alive, and she received an almighty whack to the back of the head with a rounded object—think metal piping, something like that—there's nothing to report here. The others?" He shrugged. "Won't know until I open them up, and that's just a saying. They're pretty much opened up already, except for the old lady. Kind killer, thinking of me like that, saving me a job." He smiled, laughed again, then gave his blade quick a burst of electricity. "Sorry I couldn't be more help."

"If you find anything—"

"I'll let you know. Chop-chop!" He brought the blade humming to life again and pointed to a transparent visor. "Wouldn't mind putting that on for me, would you? My hands are a bit messy."

As Langham stepped around the table to give his services, Oliver bolted from the room. How could Hank be so *jolly?* If Oliver had that job, he'd be as morose as hell. He leant against the wall in the corridor, the sinister sound of the blade rasping on his nerves.

Langham came out. "You okay?"

"I will be when we get out of here." Oliver breathed in deeply, tasting death.

"Yep, we're going now. I don't know what's up with me today, but I forgot to run a check on who owns Privo. I'll call it in to Shields, let him deal with it. I want to visit Cordelia Shields before it gets too late. Then we're calling it a day. Everything will still be here tomorrow when we wake up, still one massive fucking mess."

It was with huge relief that Oliver stepped outside into the fresh air, although faint traces of odours still lived inside his nose. That sterile room had brought it home that Louise was dead. What had he thought before then? That she was a parody of a dead body lying in the grass?

Seeing the house by the river from this distance wasn't something Oliver had thought he'd ever do, and staring at it from afar and wondering who lived inside was as close as he'd thought he would ever get. Now, standing on the semicircular, brick front step beneath the veranda, his stomach churning, he imagined what Cordelia Shields would look like.

The door swung open, the reverberating sound of the bell dying.

Cordelia Shields' face was that of someone so much younger than fifty-four. Surgery had been kind to her, smoothing out the wrinkles she'd undoubtedly have had, had she not gone under the knife. Blonde hair, salon perfect, covered her head in copious waves, some coiling on her shoulders only to continue their tumble down her chest. The ends reached below her breasts—large, augmented breasts. She sported the body of a twenty-something, well-toned and lithe. Her jogging bottoms clung to slim legs.

"Sorry to trouble you." Langham drew out his ID. "DI Langham. Would you mind talking to us about your car?"

"My car?" She frowned and brought one hand up to rest on her throat, the hand the only part of her that gave away her age. It was craggy with wrinkles. "Which *one,* darling?"

Her laugh got on Oliver's nerves.

"Your black Mercedes with the licence plate 5-H-1-3-L-D-5."

"What about it?" She smirked and arched one eyebrow, cocked her hip, leant it against the doorjamb.

Langham cleared his throat. "Who else drives it but you?"

"I don't *drive* it." She waved a hand in a dismissive manner. Pristine, long, red-polished fingernails caught a strand of her hair. "Although someone drives me *around* in it."

Ah, it was like that, was it? Definitely one of *those* people. Rich, up her own arse.

123

"When was the last time it was used?" Langham asked, his voice compact.

Oliver wondered if they were going to talk about this on the doorstep all night or whether this rude woman would actually invite them in. He was dying to sit down, even if only for five minutes. His head and broken finger ached.

"This morning. Robert took me into the city." She smiled tightly.

"Robert?"

"My driver."

"And the time before that?"

"Hmmm, let me think. Perhaps it was yesterday. Did I go out yesterday? I'm not sure. I'll have to consult my diary. Wait here one moment."

She closed the door.

"Shit. She could be doing anything in there. Warning this Robert." Langham ran a palm over his stubbled chin.

"You have a suspicious mind," Oliver said.

"I have every reason to. Especially as her car is involved in an abduction."

"Point taken."

They stood on that step, statues of impatience, waiting an interminably long time for Mrs Shields to return.

"What the fuck is she *doing* in there?" Langham muttered, the tic working beneath his eye again.

"This house is so big, she might have to walk a fair way to wherever she keeps her diary."

"Ridiculous having a house this large," Langham said. "Probably only her and a husband, a few hired help. What's the point? Why not downsize?"

Oliver disagreed. "Why *not* have it if she can? Why does she need to live in a smaller house if she can afford to live here?"

Langham looked at him as though he'd grown horns. "Are you being serious? This place should be filled with people, not one or two rattling around."

"It might have been, once. She might have had several kids, they've left the nest, and now there's just her and possibly her old man left. It's still her home. She shouldn't have to leave it, leave all the memories behind because other people think the place is too big for her."

"Other people. You mean me. Just say it."

"Yep, you. Entitled to your opinion and all that, but I don't see it the same way."

"Didn't ask you to."

"Nope, you didn't." Oliver stopped it there. He wasn't in the mood for their sniping, and the tone Langham had used meant it would be more than banter if they continued this way. "So what happens if she comes back saying she never went out yesterday or any of the days that car was spotted at Glenn's?"

Langham didn't respond. The front door swung open on well-oiled hinges, and Mrs Shields stood there again, diary in hand.

"Well, I didn't go out yesterday," she said. "I thought I had, but after looking in here, I see I have my days mixed up."

Old age crept up on you in the mind, even if your body looked younger.

"Does Robert use the car for his own purposes?" Langham cocked his head.

"No, he most certainly does not!" Indignation came off her like sleet—pointed and sharp, stinging and cold. "He lives in. I would know if he used it without my permission. Why would you ask such a thing?"

"May we come in, Mrs Shields?"

Oliver watched for her reaction. He felt she was hiding something, although he couldn't get a handle on exactly what it was.

"Is that necessary?" She pursed her mouth. Her top lip gained a row of vertical lines much like comb teeth. The Botox needed to be done again.

"It would be more comfortable..." Langham smiled.

"I would *much* rather we spoke out here." She glanced back into the house, a large foyer with gleaming white tiles and a mahogany staircase at the centre, shooting straight up to a veranda like the one outside the house. Gaze back on them, eyes wider, though she hid any anxiety well, she said, "Just tell me what the problem is and I'll deal with it. Broken back light? Did I forget to purchase new road tax? Flat tyre? What?"

Oliver wanted to laugh. She was good at this acting innocent business.

"None of those." Langham sighed, his irritation with her game obvious.

"Then what, for God's sake?" She clamped her lips closed, sucking them in so their rose hue disappeared.

Langham coughed. "How about child abduction?"

Her mouth sagged. Colour, pink as a tongue, formed rounded spots on her cheekbones. A gasp came out of her, torn, an after-thought—that gasp should have come first, shouldn't it? "Child abduction? Whatever do you *mean?*"

"Exactly what I said."

"Surely not!" She moved back a few inches. "There is no way my baby would be involved in such a thing."

"Your baby? Would that be Robert?"

She rolled her eyes, the irises disappearing for a moment, her whites blood-veined, bulging. "No! My baby! My *car!*"

"Right, Mrs Shields, I'll be frank with you. I'm tired. Very tired. I'm investigating several murders. A child is missing, taken by a man driving your *baby.* Now, either you let me in, or I call for backup." Langham glanced about. "Your neighbours...they're close enough to see your driveway. See a few patrol cars travelling up it. Is that what you want?" He shrugged. "With my car, us two standing here, we could be salesmen. Do you understand what I'm saying?"

He said that last statement like he'd spoken to a dense child.

She blinked several times. "I really don't think—"

"I don't care what you think. I am coming into your house to ask questions whether you want me to or not. Whether it's now or later, I don't care. Unless you prefer to accompany me down to the station. Would that suit you better? Of course, we would drive you, not Robert. Your car, it will have to be collected. Forensics will need to check it."

"I am telling you, Detective, my baby wouldn't transport an abducted child."

She spoke as though her car was a living being. Was she cracked in the fucking head? Oliver was losing patience with her. He had the urge to shove her into the house, march her to a sofa, and get some bloody answers.

"Your baby would have had no choice, because Robert, or a man at any rate, would have been *driving it!*" Langham snapped. "Where is Robert now?"

"I... I... He *was* here, but—"

"Convenient." Langham clenched his jaw, grinding his teeth so the muscles in his cheeks danced. "Listen, I'm not into pussyfooting around you now. I'm going to call for another officer. He will bring uniforms with him, who will have your car towed. You will speak to me and my colleague here, about the times Robert has driven your car with your knowledge. If you are so sure it hasn't been used without you in it, then you must have been present when he visited the home—several times, I might add—of the abducted girl before

128

finally taking her . Now, that girl was taken but has been able to get away from her abductor because she has *returned home and killed her parents today*." Langham bunched his fists. "We do not know where she is now, but I intend to find out. Your car was used to take her, so it isn't a far-fetched assumption that the young girl has been kept here. I have probable cause to enter this house without a warrant. Do. You. Understand. Mrs. Shields?"

"Yes. Yes! I'm not stupid!" She glanced back again.

What was she *doing?* Checking the coast was clear before she let them in? Stalling them? Oliver side-eyed Langham, who got out his phone and walked back down the drive—the only way anyone could get off the property, unless they chose to dive into the river at the rear. He barked orders, striding across the gravel, his shoes crunching—Rice Krispies in milk, amplified—his face rigid. He finished his call, features now composed, flat and expressionless.

"Mrs Shields. You're married, correct?" he asked.

"Yes." Her hand fluttered at her throat again. "But only in name. He... We're separated. Have been for quite some time." She blustered on. "I... I was building up my career. He didn't like it. He... I earned more than him. We—"

"Your husband is a police officer. A detective?"

Oliver's guts twisted. *Jesus Christ...*

"Yes." She looked back again, cheeks redder now.

"A detective currently unavailable, one on duty, who, for reasons unknown, hasn't reported in and isn't answering his phone."

Oh, fuck me...

"What has that got to do with me where he goes?" She bit her bottom lip, the flesh around her two front teeth bleaching white.

"And you are the owner of PrivoLabs, yes?"

"Yes. And what of *that?*"

"Mrs Shields, I would like to take you into the city for questioning."

"I'm under arrest?" She let her jaw drop, a pathetic attempt to look dismayed, and shook her head.

"Not yet, no. But I have a feeling you will be."

CHAPTER THIRTEEN

O fficers had arrived within minutes, oozing over the house and grounds like ants on a mission. Mrs Shields had been taken into the city, bristling and prickly as she'd been led to a police car. Oliver thought Langham's touch of having her escorted in a marked car amusing—if she was involved in this crap, she deserved to be seen, to have people know she was a criminal. A small part of him wondered whether she *could* be involved.

And what about Shields himself? He was *married* to her? Christ, he hadn't said word about that. He should have, what with PrivoLabs being in the picture. He shouldn't even be a part of the case. How had he expected to keep that quiet? It would have come to light sooner or later. And did that mean he *was* in on the abduction, in on PrivoLabs' wrongdoings? Had he remained silent about everything so he was in on the ground floor, able to know where the investigation was going so he could warn Cordelia? Was their separation a ruse?

Oliver followed Langham through the massive house, mind swimming with too many questions. "This fucking stinks."

"Yep," Langham said. "Like a bacteria-riddled turd."

They were upstairs, wending in and out of the many bedrooms, finding no Glenn Close and nothing to imply she'd been there.

"You getting anything?" Langham asked. "Any pushes from dead people?"

Oliver hadn't been taking any notice. Tiredness was probably a factor, his senses dulled, mind unable to cope with anything more than his own thoughts charging through his head. "No, but I can try."

He stood in the middle of what he assumed was a guest room, double bed in the centre, wooden wardrobe and matching beside cabinets the only other furniture. Pine, if he wasn't mistaken, varnished a deep amber that bordered on orange. It looked cheap, considering the amount of money

132

Cordelia had. He closed his eyes, clearing his mind of everything that filled it. The relief of that alone eased the ache in his shoulders, tension squirting out of his muscles, toothpaste from a tube.

It came, a voice, whisper-soft, and one he hadn't expected to hear.

"I'm outside."

"Shields?"

Langham spun around. "What the fuck? Jesus Christ. This isn't something we need at the moment, a copper being killed."

"Shh! I don't want to lose him," Oliver said.

"Well! He winds me up."

"He won't anymore, will he!"

"This is hard. Can't..."

"Hold on, Shields," Oliver said. "Relax. Concentrate only on speaking to me. Imagine you're just resting with your eyes closed, and speak, let the words come." He'd have to work hard to keep Shields with him if he wanted answers.

"Right. I'm sorry. For... I'm just sorry."

"Sod being sorry. That stuff doesn't matter anymore. Just tell me what you know."

"Cordelia, she isn't involved. Hasn't got a clue what's been going on. You hearing me okay? Is this working?"

"Yep. Go on."

"It's Robert, her new man. She passes him off as a chauffeur, not that I give a toss what he is. He's the one you want. The one who...who left me outside."

"What were you doing here?"

133

"I came to...to warn her. Went to see Mrs Roosay. She spoke to me through the letterbox. Told me the number plate of the car. I knew then...knew I should have said something about Cordelia owning Privo, that I didn't think she had it in her to be involved in something like this."

For Langham's benefit, Oliver repeated, "Mrs Rosé spoke to you through the letterbox?"

Langham blurted, "Oh, for Pete's sake!"

"Langham, testy as ever."

Oliver smiled. Then a thought struck him—hard. Ronan Dougherty had said one of the dead had lied to Oliver. Implied it had been Louise. Said the owner of Privo was the one they were after. Why had he lied? He asked Shields if he knew.

"Ronan knew about it from the start. Was friends with Robert."

"So why was Ronan killed?"

"He got greedy. Wanted more than a sixty-forty cut. He wanted the sixty. Said if he didn't get it he'd tell Cordelia the lot."

"The bastard lied to me. Anything else we need to know?"

"Glenn Close." Shields chuckled, ever the arsehole. *"She's planning on going to Mrs Roosay's later. Can't imagine the girl will harm the old woman, but you never know."*

"Shit."

Oliver quickly relayed the news to Langham, who barked orders into his phone. "Send officers to ninety-seven Bridgewater Road pretty fucking quick if someone isn't there already, and make sure you keep the old woman safe and someone sticks around to get a hold of that girl, got it?"

"So why were you kil… Why are *you* outside?"

"Robert. He told Cordelia he'd sort everything. Led me into the garden. She doesn't know I'm…like this. Thinks we were only talking. When she came in after you knocked, she stood at the patio doors, staring out at us. Was holding something. Her diary, I think. I waved, let her know everything was fine. Didn't…" A sob interrupted his speech. *"Didn't want her to know I had no control at all, that Robert had a gun on me. Pride… Always had a problem with it. Always did think I knew best. He waited until she'd gone before he pulled the trigger."*

"We didn't hear a gunshot."

"Silencer. Sounded like a puff of wind."

"Where is he now?"

"I tried to follow, after…after… He waded through the river. He had a car waiting, some bloke in it I hadn't seen before. He told me when we were speaking…said he kept the drug formula in his head, knew exactly how to get the strands made elsewhere if the shit hit the fan here. Fake passports, the lot. He'll be long gone. Private jet, so he said."

Oliver repeated the information so Langham could alert the airports, then asked Shields, "So what now? Do we have everyone except this Robert?"

"Yes, him and the man who picked him up. The ones who made the drugs had no idea what they

135

were doing. Thought it was just another part of their job."

"And the kids? Are there more than those we found in Reynolds' gran's basement?"

"No. Just them. From what I've gleaned from nosing about in this...state...you'll have Glenn soon. Unless she changes her mind about seeing Mrs Roosay."

"Who were you talking to on the phone about the case?" Oliver asked. "When we were listening?"

"The chief. I wanted him to see me as working better than Langham. I'm a bastard."

A gusty sigh blew through Oliver's mind.

Shields was gone.

Langham led the way outside, stride long and brisk. Oliver told him what Shields had said.

Langham snorted. "I'm telling you, he's having a last little laugh on me. Bloody tosser. What was he up to? After my job, was he?"

"No idea."

In the garden, Oliver stood on a stretch of patio. Officers milled about, seemingly unsure as to what they were looking for.

"Body out here," Langham shouted. "Keep searching."

The policemen were alert now they had something specific to go on. Oliver, although drained from his conversation with Shields, reached out to see if someone, anyone would give him any indication of where Shields' body was. Water, the image sharp and clear, filled his mind. It seemed to crash over his skin, cold and startling.

"The river. Reckon he's in there," he said.

Langham sped off, his vigorous pace taking him to the end of the garden in seconds. Oliver ran after him, out of breath by the time he reached him. They stared down an embankment at the river, a rushing, gambolling mass of frothy water, the current mean and unforgiving.

"Can't see a thing in this fading light," Langham complained. "And the spume isn't helping much either. What's up with that?"

"No idea."

"Well, we need to check the water out, whether we like it or not. Fuck's sake," he said, navigating the slash of embankment. "Last thing I expected was going out to find Shields' sorry arse." Langham paused to catch his breath.

Oliver stood beside him, lungs heavy from the chilly air. It was going to be a cold one tonight. Langham walked towards the bank edge, moving his head left and right.

"Shit," he said.

"What?"

"There he is." Langham bent over, hands planted on his knees, laughing.

"What's so funny? Where is he?" Oliver stared at the water, seeing nothing but rushing froth.

"There!" Langham pointed.

Oliver gazed that way. "Oh fuck."

Shields' bare arse stuck out of the water, and nothing else.

"Seems this Robert has a sense of humour," Oliver said.

"Seems he does. Wouldn't have wanted to be him, though, pulling down those trousers."

"Me neither. Bit sick, don't you think?"

"A little, but people do the strangest things." Langham used his phone, telling whoever was on the other end that they needed a SOCO team.

How the fuck had the other officers missed a great big arse poking out of the river?

Langham cut the call. "That body needs getting out of there. Photos taken. The way that river's going, it'll wash any evidence away."

"We don't even know Robert's surname," Oliver said.

"No, and that's something we need to find out." He phoned the station, ordering some desk jockey to root out the information. He slid his mobile away. "Best part of my job, that."

"What is?" Oliver stared at Shields' arse. His vision blurred, mind weary of the constant battering it'd had all day, but not before he caught sight of something he'd rather not have.

"Having someone else do the dirty work."

The call came in that one Robert Sanders and his companion, Peter Newbury, had been caught at the local airport. Robert had been a nightmare to

138

contain, his strength that of ten men. It had taken several officers to apprehend him.

It wasn't a huge airfield, more a strip of land surrounded by grass and a pitiful excuse for a control tower, which lurched to one side as though the wind had pushed it a little too hard for a little too long. He'd been taken to the station, would be left in a holding cell overnight until Langham could interview him in the morning. He didn't have time now, so he'd said—they were on their way to Mrs Rosé's, having received word that Glenn Close had been spotted at the park opposite the row of houses in her street. According to an officer hiding in Mrs Rosé's front garden, Glenn was flying high on a swing and had been for the past five minutes. So Robert Sanders had said, Glenn hadn't returned to him after she'd killed her parents, as he'd instructed. She was surrounded on all sides, officers ready to catch her in case she bolted.

"Damn shame, that, when you think about it," Langham said.

Oliver nodded, staring out of the windscreen at a now dark sky, thinking of Glenn. He saw her on a swing in his mind's eye, hair flying behind her as she surged forward, the length of it streaming over her face when she flew back. She was doing what she always should have, being a kid with no cares in the world. Except she hadn't ever had that kind of life, had she? Shitty parents had denied her the childhood she'd deserved, the pair of fuckers.

Yeah, Oliver acknowledged that his anger towards Mr and Mrs Close was probably stronger because he'd had a strained and unhappy childhood himself, knew a bit about what Glenn had gone through. Wished he'd been able to go on the swings without constantly worrying he'd be called a weird bastard or worse. And if he were honest, what they were about to walk into bothered him. He didn't want to see that kid taken away, treated like a criminal. He hoped the police who dealt with her were compassionate, understood why she'd acted as she had, that drugs had played a major part in what she'd done. It was out of his hands, probably out of Langham's, too, but at least the detective could keep tabs on her, could let Oliver know how she fared after her fate had been decided.

What had happened to the other kids? They'd been taken to the hospital, but when would they be reunited with their frantic parents? When all the tests on them had been exhausted? When it was deemed okay that they weren't a threat to society? He had no idea if any of them had killed. He hoped the only murderers were Alex Reynolds and Glenn. No other bodies had turned up, no new spirits had spoken to him, but that didn't mean sod all.

Langham parked at the end of the street farthest from the park. They got out of the car, closing their doors quietly, and Langham locked them without using his electronic key fob, just the key. The *blip-blip-blip* of it would have been too loud in the quiet street, alerting Glenn that someone was about.

They didn't need her running. This had to end. Now.

"How are you going to do this?" Oliver followed Langham across the road to the side the park was on.

"I have no clue. Instinct says to go up to her, see what she does."

Oliver widened his eyes. "What? And risk her going for you?"

"She didn't go back to Robert Sanders, so my guess is the drugs will have worn off by now."

"But what if they haven't? What if she's still crazed?"

"I don't know. Maybe I'm not thinking straight."

"At least talk to her from the other side of the fence first."

Iron railings skirted the park, enclosing it as a child's oasis, supposedly keeping them safe from running out into the path of a car on Bridgewater Road. Fences didn't stop anyone if they had a mind to do something, and from what Glenn had done, she might have a mind all right.

They came to a stop, level with that little girl coasting through the air. Two streetlamps burned brightly, illuminating the apparatus. Illuminating her. She had a glazed look about her, stare glassy, just one kid going through the motions of making the swing move. No enjoyment, nothing.

"She's come down off the high," Langham said. "Reckon I'm safe to go in?"

Oliver shook his head. "Is it wise?"

"I'll be all right, you know." Langham smiled, but he appeared tense, like he was withholding something.

"What's going on?" Oliver swallowed to wet his suddenly dry throat.

"The park's surrounded with trained marksmen."

"*What?*"

"Sounds mad, doesn't it? Guns needed for a kid. But there's no telling what state she's in, and kid or not, she's got to be taken into the city somehow. If she turns feral, well..."

Oliver held his hand up. Didn't want to hear anymore. "Right. But I'm coming with you."

"Not a good idea. You're not trained for this crap."

Oliver glanced at Glenn. She seemed to have no clue they were there.

Swing-swing-swinging. Hair whoosh-whoosh-whooshing.

"I still want to come."

"I could get in the shit for letting you."

"Yep."

"Okay, so I'll get in the shit if I have to, so long as you get the fuck away if she goes off on one, you got that?"

Langham pushed the metal gate open. The hinges protested with a whine. Oliver cautiously trailed him, gaze fixed on Glenn, who still swung high. A slight movement from her head, and she slowed, holding her legs out in front of her, pressed together, toes pointed in dirty white pumps, laces hanging.

They reminded Oliver of Louise's boots, what with the laces being undone.

He shuddered.

By the time they reached the swing, Glenn was still, feet on the ground, and she gripped the metal chains either side of her. Blood stained her— everywhere, everywhere—and he was surprised someone hadn't noticed that. Where the hell had she been since killing her parents? If someone *had* seen her, had they been stupid enough to think she was swathed in *paint?* Had they been so fixated on their own lives they hadn't seen that this kid needed help? He shook his head.

"Glenn?" he said.

She turned her head slowly, eyes the colour of a boisterous, storm-laden sky. Grey and bleak. No spark. No joy. Shit, he wanted to gather her in his arms and squeeze some love into her, let her know someone cared. Her face, Christ, it was near black with dried blood.

She stood, swivelled to face them.

Oliver did what came naturally and held out his arms.

And Glenn ran into them.

"Hold your fire!" Langham shouted.

Glenn clutched Oliver tightly about the back, the squall of her heart-wrenching sobs tearing a massive rip in his soul.

CHAPTER FOURTEEN

Oliver roused but kept his eyes closed, hoping to drop back to sleep. His pillow crackled.

He bolted upright. His chest tightened, and he found it difficult to pull in a decent breath. He cocked his head, thinking, hoping the action would help him realise what was wrong. Something was.

A wave of cold swept over him, and he settled back, drawing the quilt up to his chin. His teeth chattered, the air turning cold, and a nasty pinch in the pit of his stomach was all the proof he needed that it wasn't someone in *this* life giving him the jitters.

"Who are you?" he whispered. "What do you want?"

"I heard you're the one who can help me. You know, because I'm dead."

The voice wasn't faint or reedy, full of fear or puzzlement that the spirit had found themselves dead. No, this one was bursting with bravado, confidence, and possibly belonged to a male arsehole.

"Yeah, I was an arsehole. Still am."

Oliver didn't feel badly that he hadn't shielded his thoughts this time. It seemed to him the man would prefer honesty.

"Yep. So here's some honesty from me. Nice to finally meet you properly, Oliver."

"Who are you?" he said again.

"Alex bloody Reynolds."

He laughed—shards of glass splintering, then sandpaper on roughly hewn wood—the sound grating right on Oliver's nerves.

"Shut the fuck up," he snapped. "What do you want with me?"

"Nothing."

"Nothing? So piss off then!"

"Aww, that's no way to talk to someone who's just reaching out, wanting contact with someone he kind of knew in life. It's boring here, wherever the

fuck I am. Dark place, trees every-damn-where. And the stink! It's like rotting veg."

"You're in a bad place, Alex. You're going to wish you weren't there." He paused, then a thought struck him. "Hang on, how did you *get* there?"

"Think I was going to spend the rest of my life in prison? Fuck, no. Coward's way out for me. I don't want no dirty bastard fucking me up the arse in the shower."

"Look, tell me what you want. If you're only here to mess me about, well, don't."

"Listen, there's one more out there. Just thought you should know. One more like me, getting ready to kill right...this...minute."

His presence vanished.

Oliver sent Langham a message: THERE'S ANOTHER ONE BEING KILLED.

The unease he'd felt prior to Alex coming disappeared, but another chilling feeling took its place, white-hot in its intensity and not a pleasant sensation. Fingers of fear crept up his spine, and a strange, almost out-of-body-experience occurred. He was above a bedroom, a double divan below with a woman on it, hacked to pieces, fresh blood still dripping from a corner of the sheet that hung over the side.

"You see me? You see me there?"

Oliver nodded.

"He's only just gone. You can catch him. I followed him. He's under the bypass, the one off

Chaucer Street. He's... He's got... Oh God, he's licking my blood off his hands."

"Where do you live? Where am I? Your flat?"

"Twenty-seven Portman Street. Bungalow with a green door."

"Your name?" Oliver couldn't look at her anymore, the blonde hair streaked red, the torso, arms, and legs God knew where. Stomach gaping open, innards splayed across the bed, a bad impression of modern art.

"Sasha Morrison. He took parts of me. Has them with him. In a...black...rubbish bag."

Oliver felt her pain, that her life had been cruelly ended. "Why you? Do you know?"

"I'm the last one to know where the main man is. Who he is."

"The main man? There's another?"

"Yes. The two caught at the airport, they were just men who acted like they'd masterminded the whole thing. They worked for someone else."

"Who?"

"Gideon Davis."

"Where is he?"

"Spain."

"Oh Jesus. He runs the operation from there?"

"Yes. I... I need to go. I'm getting colder. It's...things are fading... W—"

Oliver went to call out, to ask her to hold on for a few more seconds, but he was hauled from Sasha's flat and back onto the bed.

The doorbell rang, and he rushed downstairs.

Langham stood on the doorstep. "What is it?"

Oliver babbled, leading him inside to the kitchen, spewing the last few minutes out into the air. "I can't believe he bloody killed himself."

"A lot of them do." Langham sat at the table. "They can't handle prison, yet they can handle killing people."

Oliver leant against the worktop. "It doesn't make sense. If you've got the guts to kill, why would prison worry you?"

"Because they can't kill anymore. For most of them, it's in their blood."

"But Alex was made to kill. The drugs."

"I reckon, with him, he'd have killed eventually anyway. He wasn't your average human, was he?"

"No." Oliver sighed. "You going to call Sasha's death in?"

Langham nodded and grabbed his phone. He dialled, speaking quickly, his words tripping over one another as he gave the location of the man who had killed Sasha and where they could find her body. He ended the call. "You want to come to the bypass with me?"

"Yes."

"Get dressed then. After we've rounded him up, we need to go back to the station. Someone will be alerting the Spanish police about Gideon Davis, but I've got a shitload of interviewing to do—child suspects coming out of my arse—and too many things to get sorted. Let's wrap this bloody thing up. It feels like it's been going on for days."

148

In the murky light that was predawn, Langham drew the car up to the kerb behind a string of police cars. Coppers were strategically placed along the top of the bypass and at either end of the square tunnel below. Had they been instructed to wait for Langham before they acted, or had another detective or senior officer gone down the muddy incline and discovered the killer there? Maybe the man licking blood from his hands had drawn a weapon, holding up his arrest.

Oliver followed Langham to a sergeant standing on the rise and asked, "He been arrested?"

"No. He's asleep. Thought we'd better wait for you. Knew you were coming, see."

"Right," Langham said.

They walked away from the sergeant and down the slope.

Oliver said, "Maybe they thought, because this is supposedly the last drugged-up killer out there, you'd want to be the one who brought him in."

Langham slipped on a particularly wet sheet of mud and nearly went down on his arse. "Yeah," he said over his shoulder. "But fucking hell, what if I don't want to be the one?"

"It's your job to be the one." Oliver nearly slipped on the same patch even though he'd braced himself not to. "Like it appears to be my job to listen to the dead. Not what I'd have chosen, but there you go."

They came to a stop on a path strewn with tiny pebbles, loose dirt, and a smattering of rubbish. A supermarket receipt fluttered by, the long trail of paper undulating, an eel. Someone either had a big fucking family to feed or had bought food for a party. The paper seemed to go on forever, then finally fucked off and disappeared inside the tunnel.

Oliver stared into it, stomach rolling. Beneath there, in the darkness and shadows, was a man fast asleep—asleep after butchering an innocent woman.

How do you kip after something like that? How do you live with yourself?

Langham walked ahead, approaching the tunnel on near-silent feet. He stopped to whisper to a pair of officers situated to the left and out of sight of anyone inside, nodded, then turned to face Oliver. "Stay there."

The darkness scoffed Langham and the other two officers whole, and Oliver could only hope it didn't chew them up and spit them right back out again. He didn't have to wait long. Langham's echoic voice emanated from the pitch a few seconds after a torch blared to life, the beam illuminating what looked like a heap of clothing on the ground.

"Asleep? A-fucking-*sleep?* Who the hell checked this guy? It's obvious he's sodding well dead!"

Without waiting for permission, Oliver sped into the tunnel, coming abreast of the three standing men. He stared at the corpse, its face frozen in an expression of innocence, as though the blood covering his skin was just makeup, that it didn't belong to Sasha Morrison. Had the man, a

150

vagrant by the look of him, been given the drugs on the street then told where he needed to go when the urge to kill took over him?

Bloody hell...

Something Oliver had learnt early on in life was, despite wanting something so bad and praying for it, you sometimes never got it—you know, peace, a quiet life. Langham's request to have him as an aide was accepted. Oliver had no formal police training, didn't get hunches or have any desire to actually *be* a copper—it wasn't in his blood, wasn't the thing that shoved him out of bed in the morning, ready to wade through another case, another day full of sick people with no regard for others, catching them and making sure they had a stint behind bars. Him going around with Langham more often was daunting, so the fact that the dead hadn't contacted him lately was a Godsend—it meant he hadn't been up close and personal with the harsh side of policing since Sugar Strands.

After that case had finally ended, Gideon Davis apprehended after being watched, after painstaking investigations to find evidence that had actually led the authorities to conclude he was the mastermind behind it, Oliver had been knackered beyond description.

With his sleep no longer interrupted by death's call, he spent his days well-rested and alert. He left his old job, wanting something new to do, and started a part-time position as an editor's assistant for the local rag—tea-making boy, more like—his boss agreeing that if Oliver was needed by the police in future, he could go on a moment's notice and also on the proviso that he gave reporters inside information on any high-profile cases he worked on. He'd checked with Langham on that, and Langham had said he'd give Oliver as much information as he could without compromising the investigations. Oliver's boss had been content with that.

So, all round, everything had worked out pretty well, although Oliver had a hard time keeping the images of the Sugar Strands case out of his head. Even though he'd told himself he didn't need answers, he apparently did. His subconscious asked for them when he slept, and he woke in a sweat, streams of queries flapping through his mind, same as that supermarket receipt he'd seen. There were too many victims, that was it. Too many bodies had stacked up, all owing to an arsehole named Gideon Davis, who wasn't spilling the beans on anything he'd done or why.

Before all this shit, Oliver had only had to deal with one dead body at a time—that of the spirit who contacted him—and that had been hard enough. If a dead person did manage to get a hold of him again in the future, he hoped it would be like it had always been. Just one.

He sat in the police station's public waiting area, legs open, hands between his knees, gaze fixed firmly on the needs-a-bloody-good-wash linoleum. Langham would be finishing work soon—five minutes max he'd said about half an hour ago—and they had a table booked at Grisotto's, some new Italian place in the city, where they'd catch up, stuff their guts, and enjoy a bevvy or two. He glanced up. Those behind the glass pane of the front desk milled about, some on phones, some with their heads bent over paperwork.

All he seemed good for nowadays was making tea with four sugars, filing old news stories, and listening to his boss waffle on about needing new and exciting leads, nudge-nudge, wink-wink, get the dead to speak to you, boy. Oliver sighed every time, explaining he couldn't just summon the dead people whenever he bloody felt like it.

He felt lost without the dead. Yes, when they'd contacted him in the past it had sometimes been a bind, too much for him to handle, but their silence, their utter, deafening silence was worse. As though he was useless, had no purpose.

The swoosh of the door leading to the innards of the police station had Oliver turning his head. An officer swept by, seemingly oblivious to him sitting there.

A policeman behind the desk tapped on the glass partition. "Langham's caught up in some last-minute things. Said he'll meet you at yours in about an hour."

On the walk home, he thought about the drugged kids, how they'd been reunited with their parents once they'd been given the all-clear by doctors and the police. None of them remembered who'd given them the drugs—none except Glenn Close, now living in a secure kids' home, living a good life she should have had right from the start. She was young enough that the horrors could become a distant memory if enough happy times eclipsed the bad.

As he rounded the corner, a cat zipped out of a bush, streaking across his path with a glance over its shoulder. In his house, the scent of a good old British breakfast, stale now that hours had passed since it was cooked, welcomed him in. He walked down the short, no-room-to-swing-a-cat hallway, then into the living room, where he slumped onto the sofa, a beige velour thing that squeaked with every movement. He rested his head back and closed his eyes, wondering if a court date had been settled yet for Gideon Davis. For the first time, he wanted to follow up on the bad guy, visit the public gallery and see how things went after people had been caught.

He sat like that for a long time, opening his eyes when a knock rapped on the front door.

Langham held up a six-pack. "Sorry I'm late. Finished laying the groundwork for a new case that came in when I was meant to be leaving. Still want that grub?"

"Yep. Come on, let's go and get pissed."

Oliver needed that. A good old beer sesh before the next dead person spoke to him.

He had a feeling it wouldn't be long before they did…

Printed in Poland
by Amazon Fulfillment
Poland Sp. z o.o., Wrocław

56345852R00094